I0689653

The Sweet Spot:

Your Roadmap to Maximum Confidence and Magnetism

MICHELLE BACA

Copyright © 2019 by Michelle Baca

All rights reserved.

No part of this book may be reproduced or used in any manner without written permission of the copyright owner except for the use of quotations in a book review. For more information, address: mb@michellebaca.com

www.michellebaca.com

The author of this book doesn't dispense medical advice or prescribe the use of any technique as a form of treatment for physical, emotional, or medical problems without the advice of a physician. The intent of the author is to offer information of a general nature to help you in your quest for emotional and spiritual well-being. In the event you use any of the information in this book for yourself, the author and the publisher assume no responsibility for your actions.

First paperback edition: April 2019

Cover design by Laura Duffy
Editing by Jennifer Gandin Le

ISBN: 978-1-64184-118-4 (paperback)
ISBN: 978-1-64184-119-1 (ebook)

Table of Contents

Part 3: Achieving the Sweet Spot

Introduction

I met Lynda, a fellow speaker and coach, at a conference in Costa Rica. After we'd known each other for a few years, she confessed that her initial impressions of me had been lukewarm. "You were so quiet and sweet when we met in person. I didn't realize what a powerhouse you were until I saw your social media videos and content." I understood her unstated implication: when we met in person, she thought I was nice, but forgettable.

I knew exactly what she was talking about. At the conference, I felt like the real Michelle hadn't really shown up; instead, I was the Michelle who withdraws and dilutes herself when she gets tired and overwhelmed.

It's frustrating to know that you are powerful and that you have the capacity to impact people in a powerful way — and to be an introvert. Sometimes, at the end of a conference, networking event, or party, I would leave wishing for a "do-over" because I had shut down to some degree because I was overwhelmed. As I'd drive home, I'd feel like people didn't get the chance to know me and see the badass hidden inside.

Then I learned how to feel at home in my body and to manage my energy, thoughts, and emotions. I learned how to stay more completely present in my physical and energetic body.

And everything changed.

Now, I feel like I can go anywhere — even as an introvert — knowing that I don't have to try to project confidence, get anyone to like me, or impress anyone. I just enjoy myself, revel in feeling my own energy, and interact with people in a natural, meaningful way. It's a much easier and effortless way of being.

While I often talk about being an introvert, many extroverts have confessed to me that everyone assumes they are confident just because they are outgoing and friendly, when inside they're shriveling with insecurity or feeling as if they simply are not enough. Of course, many extroverts are great at hiding it. Many use humor to cover up their lack of confidence, which often backfires, because then they feel like everyone depends on them to entertain and be the funny one.

No matter who you are, if you can learn to get out of your head, feel sensation, pleasure, and life force energy running through your body, you will feel more at home, you will feel more expressive and free, you will feel more alive — and all of this will translate to you having a powerful and magnetic presence.

When I teach people to "turn on" their magnetic energy, I tell them that initially it may seem like work, but once you get used to how good it feels, it becomes a pleasurable experience. My favorite definition of magnetism is one shared by my coach and mentor, Bo Eason, a former NFL player, stage performer, and speaker: "The power to affect others with the delight and enjoyment you take in yourself." Once I learned how to do that, I realized I could change lives, make a difference, and get noticed by simply being myself and conveying my message with pleasure.

Being magnetic is not about having a big or loud personality; it's about being yourself and enjoying the effect you have on others. Who doesn't want to feel completely alive, satisfied, and turned on by simply enjoying their body, energy, and presence?

If you're reading this book, you're probably a little like me: you're interested in presence and magnetism because you want to make a difference by impacting people. We are compassionate, loving, giving souls who want to help people believe in themselves and succeed. These traits make it common for us to focus on other people and the impact we have on them.

But you can encourage others to follow their hearts and their dreams simply by following yours and being an example. Even if you never uttered a single encouraging word, you would still have an impact by allowing others to witness how you operate in life. Sometimes, the most inspiring people are the most humble; when they hear how they have inspired others, they seem surprised. All they were doing was just being themselves.

Your Spirit Wants You to Feel Alive

Have you ever felt you were simply going through the motions in life? Have you ever felt you'd awakened in the middle of the wrong story? Is there an area in your life right now where you think you have gotten way off track?

If you've ever found yourself sleepwalking though life, you know how dark and bleak it can feel, and you know that you do not want to go back. If you are there right now, this is your wake-up call. It's time to splash some cold water on your face and start feeling alive. If you do not feel excitement, aliveness, vitality, a reason for waking up in the morning, and feelings of being "turned on" by your life — something needs to change. You need to start making a course correction.

The Crisis Wake-Up Call

People want to feel alive. This is why many people have a "mid-life crisis," though this type of crisis can happen to anyone at any time. When a person reaches a point in their lives where they feel they are simply going through the motions, they start to crave some sort of "pattern interrupt." They yearn for something new, something interesting, something that reminds them they are alive, wakes up their senses, and amps up their adrenaline.

This can happen at any point in your life where you feel bored, stuck, uninspired, without desire, or without a fire burning inside. When you've been in this place for a while and you get a glimpse of what it's like to feel fully alive again, you will likely crave more of that — whatever "that" is.

Maybe it's the sports car that gets your blood pumping and makes you feel younger. Maybe it's gambling that increases your heart rate and makes you feel like a risk-taker. Perhaps it's skydiving or having an affair with someone that turns you on in a way that you haven't felt in a while -- or ever. It could be an addiction to shopping. As the list goes on, some very destructive patterns and habits can develop. Perhaps one of the most dangerous addictions takes hold — an addiction to drugs, ecstasy, Xanax, cocaine, heroin, or something else that gives you an artificial high.

But we don't need these things in order to feel alive again. We just need to learn and practice techniques and habits that bring us back to our bodies, back to our physical selves, back to our senses. We need to move away from being lost in our own thoughts, trapped in our heads, living in the past or future, or wasting time and energy staying stuck in regret, worry, anxiety, and self-doubt.

While many people wait until a crisis to start making adjustments, there are always warning signals before this point. Our internal wisdom starts giving us signs, but we may dismiss them or tell ourselves that we'll take care of them later. All of a sudden, the minor toothache has turned into major oral surgery. While you couldn't bear to take two hours off work for a dental check-up, you're now forced to spend a few days recovering and thousands of dollars for the bigger procedure. Your internal guidance system communicates in the form of "gut" feelings, hunches, and physical and emotional clues. It will give you subtle signs at first; if you don't pay attention, it will start speaking louder and louder until perhaps it has to create a physical or mental emergency to incite action.

Learning The Language of Your Bodily Wisdom

One of the quickest ways to strengthen your intuition and develop your innate power is to familiarize yourself with your physical and energetic bodies. When you have an intimate connection with your body, mind and soul, you have access to the only guidance system you'll ever need — your own internal compass.

Learning to amplify your energy and strengthen your pleasure power center will help you feel present in the moment, make decisions, feel more energized, heal your body, and hold the space for others to feel more alive and inspired simply by being in your presence.

If you use the practices in this book to explore pleasure, radical self-love, vulnerability, and unleashing your primal power, people will respond to you. They will be attracted to you. They will want to be around you and hope to have some of your energy rub off on them. You will make a difference simply by showing up and being the example of what it feels like to be fully alive and aware of the power you possess.

Important Note:

To get the most out of this book, it's important not just to read the exercises but to put the book down and do them. Experiencing these practices in your own body, over and over, will make all the difference.

PART ONE

Waking Up!

CHAPTER 1

How Your Body Says "No"

Three months after graduating from high school, I sat in my college freshman orientation. The facilitator listed facts about the university and their specialty majors, including salary information, possible career paths for various majors, and the likelihood of being hired in the various fields of work. Because no one had told me otherwise, I assumed I was supposed to use these statistics and facts to choose my major.

For most of my life, I'd made decisions with my head, using logic and reason. Nobody ever taught me how to listen to my intuition. My schoolteachers didn't teach us how to use our instincts. We learned math, science, reading, writing, and English, but we never learned how to get in touch with our feelings, our soul desires, or our internal wisdom. There wasn't much awareness or emphasis on emotional intelligence at school or in my community. I thought decision-making was about making a list of pros and cons and figuring out what was practical, reasonable, and respectable. No one ever took me aside and showed me how to choose according to what made me smile and put a sparkle in my eyes.

I didn't know what was missing from that college orientation. If someone had asked me what I was interested in and passionate about, perhaps I would have chosen a different major. But they didn't. I chose Management Information Systems as my major because the facilitator said it was one of the fields of study with the highest paying salary. Seeing dollar signs, I made my decision based solely on the money-earning potential.

I got what I thought I wanted. Within a few months of graduating, I landed a job as Systems Analyst and Database Programmer with an impressive starting salary. I didn't realize it at the time, but I was going to be paying a big price in terms of my health and happiness for that salary.

Soon after I took a new job with an IT firm, I started getting chronic tension headaches. As time went on, they got worse, making me worry I had a serious condition or disease. I saw neurologists, I had MRI brain scans, CAT scans, and psychic readings. I consulted natural healers, shamans, specialists, acupuncturists, chiropractors — you name it, I tried it. At one point, I thought I had toxic building syndrome, because I spent 40 hours a week in a newly constructed building. The explanation was logical: if the onset of the headaches coincided with working in that building, I must be able to blame my condition on the building, or the computers, or something external.

I just kept trudging along. I learned to perform my duties while constant pressure thudded in the front of my head. In my spare time, I researched possible causes and possible cures, hoping to find an answer. When I got married and left for my honeymoon, I hoped that because I was away from the office, computers, and work that I would feel great again. But I didn't. Was it a sign that I wasn't on the right career path?

I had no clue. I just felt hopeless and a little sorry for myself as I wondered if this was all there was to life.

About five-and-a-half years into my zero-passion work in the Information Technology field, the company I was working for went bankrupt. While my coworkers freaked out, I was shocked to find that I was happy. The change felt like a signal from the Universe to explore other career options. I hadn't been courageous enough to leave my job out of the blue, so this was a gift — a chance to step in the right direction.

While it was several years before I would encounter one of my most influential mentors, author Jack Canfield, and the work that would change my life, I was starting to listen to the clues. I began to embrace making choices that others might have deemed impractical or unproductive. I started taking walks around the park and visiting museums and bookstores. I took photography classes and considered a career as a photographer, not caring that I would likely take a big salary cut at first.

Despite being unemployed after the company closed, I was bursting with excitement and possibility. I wanted to share it with everyone — from my husband to strangers sitting next to me in the dentist's waiting room.

Soon after, my husband and I attended a fancy New Year's Eve dinner with several other couples. It was the new year, and I was exuberant with new plans, new beginnings — the party felt like the perfect space to talk about this moment in my life when I was ready to pursue something new and different.

I was seated across from Dana, a very blonde, pretty, polished, and poised acquaintance. She asked me about work, so I obligingly told her about losing my job because of the company's bankruptcy. Then my voice perked up and my eyes sparkled as I shared my decision to do something completely different, something outside the information technology world. I opened my heart, fully expecting her to share my excitement.

But her eyes did not light up. In fact, she squinted and glared at me. While her words were civil, her undertone was pointed: *Are you crazy? What are you thinking? You studied for four years at university, you are qualified for a high-powered job, you were making great money doing it, and now you just want to throw that all away and start from scratch?*

That's the stupidest idea I've ever heard.

Her words and energy hit me where it mattered. I let it sink in. I barely knew her, yet her words made me question what I was doing. What if everyone was thinking the same thing, and she was just the only one brave enough to say it to my face? Did my close friends and family think I was crazy, too? As the night continued, I withdrew both mentally and physically. I closed up in my body, kept my arms close to my sides, and didn't say much.

Thank goodness I didn't dwell on that line of thinking for too long. Did she look like someone who was happy? No. Was she a fun person to be with? No. Did I want to be like her? No. So why in the world would I listen to her?

What a blessing, then, to encounter an old family friend just days later with whom I had the courage to share my excitement and secret desire to become a photographer. Her response was the opposite from Dana's. She said, "Of course you can be a photographer. You can be anything you want." Her words weren't what made me smile inside. It was that I could tell she really meant it. She wasn't just being nice. I could feel her excitement and rock-solid belief that I could and should do whatever I desired.

I wish I could tell you that I found my dream work immediately, but I didn't. It took time, and I tried to play it safe by seeking a "transition" job in IT while I figured out what I wanted to do instead. But I walked into those interviews half-heartedly, and I didn't get any of them — probably because

I was unconsciously sabotaging my interviews with my indifference about the jobs. My spirit and my soul were "on guard," trying to protect me from work that would kill my spirit, give me headaches, and possibly eventually kill me.

After working with a life coach and realizing I could become a coach myself, I got my coaching certification. As I became a life and career coach and worked with others, I began to learn how to listen, to pay attention to the language of my soul. I was starting to understand that my wants, preferences, and interests didn't simply exist just for fun — they were indicators of my life path and purpose.

And the headaches ended up going away. After I was out of the work that was killing my spirit, miraculously the headaches disappeared. As it turns out, I didn't have a brain condition. There was no physical cause for my pain. It was an emotional cause. An accurate spiritual diagnosis would have been: lack of joy, lack of passion, lack of purpose, lack of intensity, lack of pleasure, and/or lack of excitement.

In hindsight, I saw that my "higher self," or my intuition, had been trying to get my attention. It wasn't the computer screens, the building, or a brain tumor. My body was trying to tell me, "No!" My body knew I was off track, but I didn't know how to read the signs.

Step Away From the Wall

I stood upside down, perched on my head in the middle of a hotel gym in Los Angeles. From this different perspective, everything felt and looked different — colors were more vivid, the light was clearer, and the world seemed more invigorating.

Not only was I seeing things differently, I felt different too. My physical and energetic strength flowed through me unimpeded, and my senses had been sparked alive. Until that moment, when I practiced my headstand at home or in the yoga studio, I'd stayed close to the wall, not sure I could maintain the pose and support myself without the wall to catch me.

I realized that I had been approaching my life the same way: tentatively, afraid of falling. I was willing to dip my toe in and try something, but I was never so sure about anything that I'd step away from the wall and trust myself completely.

I'd been coaching for about five years, but I was still searching for that magic bullet, trying different teachers, systems and techniques, in search of that miracle cure that would motivate me and skyrocket my career. While I enjoyed my work, I knew I could be doing better. I second-guessed myself at every turn, and had a hard time making things happen. I spent so much time waiting for the perfect moment or conditions, instead of showing up with confidence, ready to take action. I was surrounded by people who took risks putting themselves and their messages out in the world, and I was jealous of them. I wanted people to like me, so I was playing safe, sharing messages that I knew were relatively safe, even if they were also lukewarm.

I had no idea that the Universe had brought me here, not to learn from the man whose conference this was, but to hear from one of the speakers that he brought in instead.

An hour before, I'd been sitting in the ballroom upstairs listening, for the first time, to Jack Canfield speak, a man who would later become my teacher and mentor.

From the moment he stepped on the stage, my eyes lit up, I sat up taller and my body hummed with energy. I scribbled furiously in my notebook, trying to capture his every word. When he finished, motivation, excitement, and energy coursed through me. My mind had heard and resonated with his stories, but more than that, my body had come alive. My whole system vibrated. What he was saying struck me on an energetic level, beyond my brain's agreement with his words. My body was trying to tell me something.

I went back to my room, but instead of changing into pajamas, ordering room service, and decompressing from the day, as I usually did at conferences, I changed into my workout gear and took the elevator down to the gym.

Vibrant energy flowed through my veins. I felt as if I'd discovered a new, natural drug. It streamed through my body, and there I was — completing a headstand unlike any I'd ever done before. Jack had helped stir up in me some of the vital life-force energy that enables people to do things that are extraordinary or outside of their comfort zones.

I didn't know it at the time, but my body was trying to tell me I was on the right track, that I should move mountains to immerse myself deeper into that kind of energy.

I listened. I began paying attention to what inspired me and made me light up. I began to see how my physical body reacted when I was onto something good. When I was on the right track, not only was I in a positive state of mind, but the rest of my body became engaged and involved. My heart raced just enough to make me feel excited, my eyes widened, my eyesight sharpened, and my pleasure power center warmed and tingled. I could do things I thought I couldn't do, both physically and mentally.

My body was also showing me that incredible shifts in mindset, attitude, motivation, ability, and energy didn't have to take weeks, months, and years — they could occur in just minutes or seconds, like flipping a switch.

How Your Body Says "Yes"

Sounds of the ocean floated through the air as I sat in the gorgeous hotel patio. It was the first time I'd attended a conference breakout session in the open air. It was hot and humid, but as dusk approached, the air was beginning to cool. With such beautiful surroundings, I wondered if we would be able to pay attention.

As soon as the speaker began, I knew I didn't have to worry about focus. The speaker, a Tantra teacher and sex coach, spoke about finding the courage and power to break the chains that were holding us back. When I first heard about Tantra, I thought that it was primarily a spiritual approach to sex. But the more I learned, the more I realized that it is much more than that. It is about learning to embrace the body as a sacred vehicle that should be honored and celebrated. It is also about getting in touch with our spirits, our energy, our breath, and our connection to all living things as a way to heighten our awareness and ability to be present and experience pleasure in our daily existence. You don't need a partner to practice Tantra; all you need is your awareness, an interest in increasing your connection to yourself, and a sense of wonderment about how miraculous our bodies are and how beautiful life is.

I realized that while I had had liberated myself from the restraints of my previous career, I had new chains to address. Breaking through barriers isn't something you only do once in your life. As you evolve, you'll need to expand your potential and open yourself up to more pleasure and fulfillment by becoming aware of any new shackles that have wrapped themselves around you. As the waves crashed on the shore in the distance, I acknowledged how far I had come, yet I also longed to take my evolution to the next level.

While I enjoyed the corporate workshops I taught, I suddenly knew I could take my business in a new, sexier, more fun and expressive direction. I wanted to help people experience feeling alive and "turned on" by getting out of their heads and connecting with their bodies and capacity to experience pleasure and aliveness.

No one had ever taught me that connecting to your sexual energy could be a form of personal development and could help me to increase my vitality, drive, and enthusiasm. But I realized that when I felt sexy, I felt powerful. Years before, I had taught sessions to burnt-out people in the workforce to help them find their passion, but I had never made the connection between sexual energy and passion about your work.

During the session, I imagined what it would feel like to stand up there and teach a session like this myself. My workshops were never this much fun! Somewhere along the way, I had gotten the idea that speaking and teaching were serious and required hard work. What if I could facilitate workshops that felt like fun instead of work, and achieved even better results? I craved more playfulness in my life and work. I wanted to do be doing what she was doing.

Through movement, breath and partner work, and dance during the session, we awakened a powerful energy that began to radiate through our bodies. Walking out of that session and into an extended course of study with the teacher was when I committed to helping people like me — those of us who tend to think too much — find an easy, quick, pleasurable way to break free from the cycle of over-thinking and spending too little time feeling engaged and expressive.

In the bathroom after the session, I looked in the mirror while I washed my hands. The woman looking back at me seemed five years younger than the one who walked into that session. My eyes were brighter, my skin more radiant. How was this possible? I didn't know. But I trusted it. It was like I had discovered a secret.

At dinner that evening, I approached the teacher and told her how amazing I felt after doing the work with her. She said, "There you are. Now I can see you." I understood that when she encountered me before the session, I was almost invisible because I had my guard up, which made it impossible for her to see the real me behind the walls I had put up. Her reaction, combined with the sensations in my body, told me this is how I wanted to show up in the world: saying yes to feeling alive and turning myself on whenever I wanted to.

For people like me who may never have considered themselves creative, expressive, brave, sexy, or powerful, it can sometimes feel like those qualities are beyond our reach — we weren't born with them, so it feels impossible to emerge from our shells and live out loud. But having the desire to bring out those qualities in yourself is enough to light the spark.

Flipping the Switch

During those 75 minutes in Costa Rica, I was able to shift my energy drastically. I felt more energy, motivation, vibrancy, mojo, and aliveness after that 75-minute session than I had felt in more than 16 years of mindset work. You can shift your energy in minutes; even seconds.

Imagine you're at home having an argument with a family member. Things are a little heated and tempers are flaring, so you speak in a loud, upset voice. Then the phone rings: it's a colleague whose call you need to answer. In the midst of your yelling, you pick up the phone and cheerfully say, "Hello" and carry on a polite, friendly conversation.

You make a choice about what sort of energetic state in which you are going to show up. This is proof that you can control your energy.

Think back to when you were a child. Was there ever a time when you convinced your parents to let you stay home from school with a mild illness? Did you ever notice that right around three o'clock in the afternoon, when school was over, you'd magically begin feeling much better? Even though you'd been sick in bed all day, suddenly you felt like you might even be able to go play outside. There was now no way your parents could make you go to school because it was over! This new possibility of being able to walk, run, and play happened quickly. Your energetic state shifted in a matter of minutes. Did anything change physically? Probably not. The difference was in your mindset and in your energy.

Your mindset and energy are under your control; you can use them to flip the switch and tune yourself into a higher energy frequency.

You learn to flip the switch by getting good at recognizing how your body says "Yes" and how it says "No."

EXERCISE: YOUR BODY'S "NO"

Recall a time in your life when you felt mentally and emotionally drained. What was happening in your life? Where were you? How did you feel physically? Mentally? Emotionally?

Close your eyes and recall how you felt in as much vivid detail as possible. Take a physical and energetic snapshot of what this felt like.

Who is the most negative person you know?

Close your eyes and imagine being stuck in a room with this person and take mental notes about how your body reacts, memorizing the physical sensations.

Think of a time in your life when you felt the least empowered.

Close your eyes and take an inventory of your thoughts, emotions, and physical state. Take a physical and energetic snapshot of what being powerless feels like.

Recall in vivid detail your most embarrassing moment. Close your eyes and put yourself back there. Memorize what this overwhelming feeling of embarrassment feels like.

Think of a time when you were physically ill.

Close your eyes and capture what emotions, thoughts, and physical sensations are present when you are experiencing illness in your body.

It's helpful to memorize what it feels like in your mind, body, and energetic field to be affected by negativity and weak energy so that when you recognize that feeling, you can use that as a cue to shift into a higher vibration state.

> *Practice catching yourself when you slip into an uninspired state. Once you can catch yourself, you can start to recall the opposite feelings, thoughts, and emotions, the ones that leave you feeling turned-on, inspired, and uplifted.*
>
> *Now, let's practice learning the language of how your body says "Yes."*

EXERCISE: YOUR BODY'S "YES"

Recall a high-energy time in your life when you were so "in the zone," you even surprised yourself. Close your eyes and take a moment to soak in everything about the way you felt, the way you were moving, the way you were talking, and how you felt in your body. Take a physical and energetic snapshot of what this feels like.

What is something that always lightens the mood for you and makes you laugh?

Take a moment to close your eyes and transport yourself to this place of lightness and playfulness. Take a physical and energetic snapshot of what this feels like.

Imagine that you are listening to your favorite music. What is it? How does it make you feel?

With your eyes closed, hear and feel the music and notice what it does to your physical and energetic bodies. Take a snapshot of how you feel in your body when listening to this music.

Who is the most inspiring person you know?

Close your eyes and imagine being in this person's presence right now. Take a physical and energetic snapshot of what being in this person's presence feels like.

What is your favorite thing to do during your free time?

Close your eyes and use your imagination to visualize that you are indulging in this activity. Memorize what it feels like when you engage in this activity.

Recall the biggest success in your life.

> *Close your eyes and recall how you felt in as much vivid detail as possible. Describe what feelings, physical sensations, and emotions come up for you when you take yourself back to that triumphant state. Take a physical and energetic snapshot of what this experience felt like.*
>
> *What rituals, habits, exercises, or practice help you get into a high-vibration state?*
>
> *With your eyes closed, imagine that you have just completed a session filled with your favorite rituals, practices, and exercises and notice what feelings and sensations this produces in your body and in your mind.*
>
> *Visualize a person whom you find attractive and has a high level of magnetism; just seeing them can turn you on.*
>
> *Take note of what simply thinking about this person does to your body and which emotional and physical sensations are triggered.*

Chances are that immersing yourself in these questions and writing down your answers made you feel happier, lighter, brighter, and more alive, even if you didn't actually write your answers down or close your eyes and visualize anything.

You can shift your energetic state relatively quickly. Your mind is powerful. Simply thinking about positive, inspiring, and uplifting people, situations, and experiences can shift your physical and energetic state. It's the same as your mouth watering when you think about a juicy lemon: the thoughts and memories trigger feelings in your body.

CHAPTER 2

Your Life-Force Energy

Most people really aren't "in their bodies." Most of their energy is in the mental realm, not the physical realm of sensory experience. They are "in their heads," thinking, over-thinking, worrying, analyzing, regretting, forecasting, second-guessing, blaming, and agonizing. If we can dedicate time to figuring out how to *"think less and feel more,"* we will be more likely to enter the state of feeling turned on that we practiced reproducing in Chapter 1.

Connecting with your physical body has a way of snapping you back to reality and the present moment. Shaking up our senses brings us back to our bodies.

Sometimes it's startling — someone physically touches you and you practically jump out of your skin with surprise. This dramatic reaction typically happens when we are "somewhere else" in our heads, lost in thought, and the touch startles us back into our physical selves.

"Frisson" is a French word that translates in English to "shiver." The sensation is similar to getting chills or goosebumps, but is usually caused by a stimulus other than a cold environment. It is typically experienced as part of an intense emotional reaction to something like music, vivid imagery, or touching words or memories. It can feel extremely pleasurable because it is a perfect reminder of our aliveness.

Frisson is amazing when it happens unexpectedly, but you don't have to wait for it — you can create these feel-good sensations in your body any time you want. In this chapter, you will practice doing so by exploring your senses. You will use your senses and your life-force energy to wake yourself using sound, sight, smell, taste, touch and your awareness of your life-force energy.

Moving, powerful music works wonders for many people who need to relax and calm down when they have too much mental stimulation, nervousness, or anxiety. Going for a drive while singing and listening to your favorite songs can calm your nervous system and raise your vibration. And it feels even better when you sing along, engaging your voice and your hearing in unison.

I like to smell my coffee or wine before I take a sip to experience more sensual pleasure from the moment. When I'm out shopping and I see a throw blanket or pillow that looks soft and plush, I run my fingers over it as I pass by. As I'm walking or driving, I like to practice appreciating the sky and landscapes as natural, visual artistry.

When I ask people what they want, more energy is almost always at the top of the list. *I want more energy to enjoy my life, to enjoy my relationships, to pursue the opportunities that I am interested in, to do my household chores, to complete my work, to play with my family, to engage in sports activities and hobbies, to exercise so that I have a healthy body.*

Learning to use your senses and life-force energy can become your most effective natural energy booster. Becoming aware of it and learning how to help direct its flow throughout your physical and energetic body is the quickest, most enjoyable way to turn on your magnetism, enjoyment, pleasure, and productivity. There exists an elegant spiral — when you connect to your life-force energy using your senses, you feel more alive. And when you feel more alive and notice what your energy feels like coursing through your body, you increase your awareness of your life-force energy, which increases your energy.

Energetic Presence

Let's tune into heightening your awareness of the energy inside your body and the energy radiating outside your body. You might know it as your aura or astral body; for our purposes, think of it as your energetic presence.

Your energetic presence is the tingling and vibration that radiates off your skin and inside your body when you put your attention on it. Your energetic presence flows throughout your body and around the edge of your skin, radiating off your body about an arm's length around you in all directions.

> **EXERCISE: PRACTICE SENSING YOUR OWN ENERGY**
>
> *Take at least three deep breaths. As you do this, make sure that when you inhale, you breathe all the way down into your abdomen so that it expands, in addition to your chest. This is the best way to know you're taking a deep enough breath.*
>
> *As you exhale, imagine that any busy, distracting energy in your body is starting to settle in the lower half of your torso. Picture that you are drawing energy down, similar to the way*

that specks of snow in a snow globe begin to settle after you stop shaking it and set it down. Imagine that the busy, nervous energy in your body is like those snowflakes, starting to settle into the lower part of your torso, and then flow down into your legs and out through the bottoms of your feet.

Then, feel your feet planted firmly on the ground and imagine that you have roots extended out of your feet and into the ground at least one hundred feet down so that you can remain centered and grounded throughout this exercise.

One of the simplest ways to begin getting more familiar with your own life force energy is to feel the energy between your hands. Rub your hands vigorously to tune in and activate your energetic presence. When you rub your hands together relatively quickly, you will start to generate heat. Continue — feel the heat and sensations that start to build between and surrounding your hands.

Firmly clap your hands together three times, then rub them together vigorously for about twenty seconds. The friction should generate heat; you're beginning to build up energy as well. Simply by doing this movement and focusing your awareness on your hands, you're beginning to bring a sense of aliveness to them. When you are done, pull your hands slightly apart so that you can feel the magnetic energy between them. Start slowly, expanding your slightly-cupped hands away from each other as if you were holding an invisible ball. In fact, you are; this is an invisible ball of your own energy. Begin by bringing your hands about four inches away from each other, palms facing each other, noticing what you feel between them. Play with pulling your hands apart gently and then bringing them close together to play with and mold your own energy. Move as if you have the ability to magically increase and decrease the size of this energy ball. (Spoiler alert: you do!) You may feel a pulling or magnetic sensation, tingling, or like a rubber band that keeps your hands connected. Continue to play with your energy ball, seeing if you can create one about the size of a basketball. Then bring it in closer, about the size of a softball. Continue this practice as long as you enjoy the feeling of the energy that you are generating. Take a moment to feel the energy and heat that is present between your hands.

Begin to notice that this energy is also present on the outsides of your hands, along your arms, your torso, your legs, feet, and head. It radiates from you in all directions.

Your aliveness lives not only inside of your body — in your tongue, your mouth and your hands — it lives beyond them as well. Your energetic body extends out from you about an arm's width away from your physical body in every direction. Once you get good at feeling the aliveness in your hands, challenge yourself to feel it around other parts of your body as well. It helps to start with the parts of our bodies that are most sensitive; long periods of disconnection or disassociation from our bodies can leave residual numbness, even after we begin to wake up. So, we can start with the tongue, the tips of the fingers, the toes, and the hands.

Return to holding your basketball-sized energy ball. (If you need to, rub your hands together again to generate heat and become present to your energy again.) Play with expanding this energy ball out even further, eventually dropping your hands and arms and expanding the energy ball until it surrounds your entire body, extending just beyond an arm's length around you in every direction. Take a few moments with your eyes closed to enjoy being encircled by your own energy and vibration.

Radiating Your Magnetic Energy

Once you're able to construct and visualize this energetic sphere around you, you can begin to focus on what it feels like to fully occupy this space and magnify the intensity of this energy. You can imagine that this sphere is like a light bulb on a dimmer switch that allows you to increase or decrease its intensity. Experiment with turning up the intensity of your light and notice how this makes you feel. Practice turning it all the way up, lowering it back down about midway, and then turning it off or dimming it as much as possible. This will help you remember that you can have more control over your energetic presence than you might think.

Just like a light bulb, you can light up an entire room while still keeping your light within your arm's-length sphere. Glass surrounds the filament of a lightbulb to contain the energy, just like your light sphere, and this container doesn't prevent it from radiating light outward. Remembering how a lightbulb works helps me to remember that I don't have to try so hard to push my energy out into a room to have an impact and to light it up. I can have a positive effect on the energy in the room simply by being aware of my own energy and turning up the switch whenever I want, without having to worry about my energy spilling out and overwhelming people.

Your energetic presence exists everywhere inside your body and it has since you were born — you just may not have known how to put your attention on it yet. The good news is that by simply tuning into and enjoying your energetic presence, you will feel more present in the moment and more connected with your body, which naturally takes you "out of your head." For most of us, this is a wonderful escape from our default mode of dwelling primarily in our mind space. It can almost feel like a guilty pleasure, but it should be pleasurable to enjoy your own body!

EXERCISE: CREATE YOUR SPHERE OF ENERGY PROTECTION

Practice reactivating your energetic sphere that extends out and around you at least an arm's length away in all directions from your body. Allow yourself to fully occupy this space and this time, pay special attention to the edge of this ball of energy that surrounds you. Check to see if there are any gaps or cracks in the edges so that you can seal them to enhance your ability to protect your own energetic space and allow you to remain strong in your own energetic field. This will allow you to communicate articulately and remain grounded throughout your interactions. Imagine that the edges are strong and that no negative vibrations can enter your energetic space. You are constructing a bubble of energetic protection all around you. Notice what it feels like to sit in this space of freedom and protection. Do you feel like you have more room to breathe?

Now, imagine that on the outer edges of this protective energy sphere hang outward-facing mirrors. These mirrors serve to reflect any negative energy, thoughts, or intentions away from you. Imagine that you are encased in a beautiful disco ball of energy.

The real beauty of this is that you can take this energetic disco ball of protection with you anywhere!

Contain Your Energy

While many people that I work with need to expand and radiate their energy to exude more presence and confidence, some people, especially those who are sometimes told that they are "too much" or that they are intimidating, benefit from learning to contain and direct their energy.

When your energy field is not contained, people can sense your energy spilling out and entering into their energetic space, causing them to feel uncomfortable or intruded upon.

To prevent this reaction, you can practice containing your energy by paying particular attention to the edges of your light sphere. Using your awareness and imagination, check to see if the edges are strong and secure. If they're not, use your imagination to fill in any cracks and make the edges stronger and unbroken.

Practicing sensing your energy and energetically protecting yourself is essential to being able to remain powerfully calm and grounded during real-life situations.

Other Methods for Waking Up Your Body by Feeling Your Own Energy:

Feather-Light Touch

Start by using the tips of your fingers to lightly sweep over your inner arms, starting with your forearm. See if you can create the frisson response or chills for yourself. Then begin to extend your caresses to your upper arms. Don't rush — eventually make your way to your upper chest area, then explore your neck. Return to your chest and use your feather-light touch on your breasts or chest, making circling motions. If you are clothed, it is fine to sweep your fingers over your garments using slightly more pressure than you would on your bare skin. During the times of your practice when you are not clothed, you can continue your pleasure exploration to include circling, touching, and eventually lightly pinching your nipples as you progress.

Pleasure begins with your senses. Activating your senses brings you into full presence with yourself and others, which makes you more impactful in your communications and interactions.

Whole Body Tapping

You've probably heard people say they need to pinch themselves because they feel like they're dreaming. Pinching yourself actually does bring you back to your body and back to the present moment, which is also why you sometimes see people in the movies slap someone to get them to become present if they are lost in a rant or off in "space" somewhere.

You don't have to pinch yourself to wake up your body and tune in to the life force energy circulating throughout you. You can use a much more delicate and pleasurable practice: whole body tapping. Depending on which part of your body you're touching, you can use your fingertips, palms, selected fingers, or your entire hand to tap your body using varying amounts of pressure depending on your preferences and using your intuition about what your body needs. I will often start tapping the top of my head to wake up my upper energy centers and welcome divine guidance, then I'll work my way down my forehead, face, jaw, back of my neck, shoulders, chest, lower back, solar plexus, abdomen, arms, legs, and feet. I like to spend extra time tapping in my lower abdominal area where my pleasure power center is located (approximately two inches below the navel for men and two and half to three inches below the navel for women) as well as on my solar plexus (between the heart and the belly button.)

When tapping your shoulders and upper back, do not be afraid to tap using a lot of pressure. We tend to hold a lot of tension in our neck and shoulders; tapping here can help relieve some tension and dismiss negative, tense, stagnant energy. Tapping your chest can release stuck emotions and open your heart energetically so that you can project a warm radiance as well as a powerful presence. Tapping on your back where your kidneys and adrenal glands live will also help stimulate those organs and increase your natural ability to detoxify your body.

Using Your Senses Intentionally

It is easy to take our senses for granted, because we are used to relying on them for survival by alerting us to possible life-threatening situations. They work for us even when we don't think about them, but when we use them intentionally in the service of our life-force energy, their value becomes immeasurable. Your senses are important allies as you become increasingly aware of your life-force energy. They connect you to your body, creating pleasure and developing the kind of vibrational existence that raises eyebrows and draws attention.

Our senses allow us to experience the kind of aliveness that is distinct from simply basic survival. Without our senses, it would be difficult to fully appreciate the most exhilarating moments in our lives.

EXERCISE: GREETING YOUR SENSES

Begin in a seated position and focus solely on the feel of the air coming in and out of your nose as you breathe for five breaths.

Direct your attention to the sounds you hear around you and focus on the farthest sound you can hear. Listen for five breaths to that farthest sound.

Move your attention now to pick up any smells that you can sense in your environment. Inhale and exhale as you identify an individual smell or smells around you for five breaths.

Now focus all of your energy and attention on the inside of your mouth. Feel your tongue, notice how much saliva production you are experiencing and notice any particular tastes that you can sense on your tongue and in your mouth.

Next, focus on your hands, particularly on each individual finger on each hand. Visualize the underlying bones and tendons. Appreciate the way your fingers are separate, yet they are

> *also connected and work together. Feel as much sensation and aliveness in your fingers and in your hands as you can. Pay as much attention to the outside of your skin, including the grooves on your skin that make up your fingerprints, as you do to the internal components of your hands. Your hands are the second most sensitive part of your body.*
>
> *Now put everything together as you hear the farthest sound, taste the tastes in your mouth, smell your surroundings, and feel every part of your fingers and hand at the same time. Close your eyes and notice what it feels like to activate these senses all at once. Take five breaths.*
>
> *Then open your eyes and simply allow the first thing that comes into your line of vision to come to you, rather than energetically reaching out with your eyes to see. Allow things to come to you visually without necessarily seeking them out or expending energy to use your eyes to look.*

Exploring Your Senses

Smelling

Essential oils work in a way similar to touch: using our powerful sense of smell, they bring you back to the feelings inside of your body, taking you further away from your distracting thoughts. Inhaling scents deeply also naturally encourages deeper breathing. Perhaps this is where the smelling the roses part of "stop and smell the roses" came from. Deep breathing helps us slow down, go inward, and calm our nervous systems.

Essential oils, candles, and fresh flowers can enhance your mood and wake up your body. There are certain essential oils, for example, that tend to really wake you up and energize you, such as lemon, peppermint, citrus, eucalyptus, and rosemary oils. Take the time to incorporate your favorite scents into your daily life.

Seeing

You can shift into appreciating what you see more fully, letting people, places, and things enter your visual awareness without strain or stress or judgment, all of which can drain your life-force energy. This change keeps your life-force energy within your own physical body. Relax your eye sockets and allow the visual input around you to simply exist as it comes into your visual awareness. Dream boards are an example of using vision to harness your life energy — through sight, they allow us to feel something in our bodies as we contemplate our dreams and goals.

Hearing

We can wake up our senses by listening to the kind of music that speaks to us the most. Music is incredibly powerful. It has the power to create emotion, to stimulate our memories, and to make us feel good. Movie producers know this well: they insert music at the perfect points to make us feel the desired emotion. When they want us to be rife with anticipation, the perfect accompanying music is there. When they want us to feel triumphant along with the characters, they insert a ballad and our hearts soar. And when they want us to cry, even a few bars of music can send streams of tears running down our cheeks.

Take the time to collect and organize the music that speaks to your soul and evokes the emotions you want to feel. Use music as a tool — be your own musical movie director, paying serious attention to the soundtrack you want for your life.

Tasting

Many of us have conflicted relationships with food: from eating disorders like anorexia, bulimia, or orthorexia to mixed messages from society, we've lost touch with what it is to allow ourselves to be nurtured by our sense of taste. To heal our bodies and our life energy, we can choose to savor our food; we can consciously eat very slowly, enjoying the process and putting as much attention as we can on our sense of taste. One simple exercise is to eat a strawberry very slowly, sweeping it over your lips before you let your tongue touch it. Before you let it enter your mouth, before your teeth touch or pierce it, extend the experience by licking it. Then, slowly and deliberately sink your teeth into the first juicy bite, chewing it slowly, feeling it in your mouth, sensing that your mouth is watering and responding to the tastes and the texture. Finally, enjoy swallowing it into your body where you will receive the nutrients, giving thoughts and smiles of gratitude. Ahhh… and to think that was just the first bite.

Normally, we don't have this heightened level of sensation in our mouths, so this is a great experiment in noticing the difference between feeling truly alive in a certain part of your body.

When we make our taste buds happy, we typically feel better and "happy signals" are sent to our brains. Perhaps this is why people turn to food to mask the pain and to make them feel better when they're feeling down. It's the drug of choice for so many because there are so many foods that just taste so good. But most people eat too fast and don't really savor their food, thereby failing to take full advantage of the positive effects of activating our sense of taste to create feelings of "aliveness."

Moving

Moving your body wakes things up and shakes things up. Just as you practiced circulating the energy throughout your hands and body, you can experiment with sensing this energy and aliveness in your body parts while you move them through the air. Feel what it's like to play with and move your energy around through movement, especially slow, intentional dance movements. Create waves and shapes with your hands, arms, legs, head, and hips and pay attention to how your energy moves with you. Dance, exercise, play sports, practice yoga, learn Tai Chi or Chi Gong. Experiment and try new things until you find what works best for waking you up and shaking you up.

Combining Senses

What's better than activating one of your senses? Adding in another. This is why it makes sense that some people like to incorporate foods like whipped cream, chocolate, caramel, or strawberries into their sex and foreplay activity. The more senses you are aware of, the more likely the stimulus will overwhelm your system in a good way, bringing you fully present in your body and out of your thinking mind. It's a lovely escape for people who spend most of their time, thinking, worrying, analyzing, regretting forecasting, or wondering.

EXERCISE: SEXY STARFISH

Remember that all the vibrant life-force energy that composes your energy light sphere also runs throughout the inside of your body. If you ever start to lose connection with your energetic field, or become overwhelmed with your senses, bring yourself back to your physical body and the sensations of vibration and aliveness that you can feel internally. The starfish practice was taught to me by my movement coach and will help you focus on your own energy as well as increase your energy level and ability to radiate your energetic presence. What makes this practice so sexy as well as energizing is that we are going to practice radiating energy out into our limbs from our hot, fiery pleasure power center to experience what it feels like to circulate this sensual, powerful energy into other parts of our bodies.

Practice this now. For a few moments, don't worry about your light sphere and instead focus primarily on how you feel inside of your body,

If possible, begin in a standing position, with your feet in a wide stance and your arms stretching straight and out and above your head, like you are making a letter "X" with your body.

Imagine that you are a starfish; your arms and legs are your tentacles. The starfish is a beautiful and mesmerizing creature with a strong center and strength and energy radiating out from the center core out to its various arms, allowing it to use all its body as it moves.

Bring your attention to your center of gravity, which is approximately two to two and a half inches below your navel. With your eyes closed, visualize energy radiating out from your center point of gravity, or your pleasure power center as we will often refer to it throughout this book, and send energy out to your strong yet flexible starfish arms and legs. Imagine that your pleasure power center is like a fire hydrant pumping energy instead of water, gushing it out and distributing it throughout your body.

I like to pretend that I am carbonating my body with bubbles of energy, like a fizzy beverage.

Now, let your arms down, slowly resting them comfortably while maintaining the aliveness and expansion that was present when they were outstretched.

Use this practice anytime you want to feel more energized and connected to your body.

CHAPTER 3

Taking The Energy With You

It's Your Magic

It's amazing when someone brings out the magic in us, making us feel special, inspired, and confident, but inevitably, the feelings they invoked begin to fade. We forget the exact words they used. We forget what their voice sounded like when they said it. The vivid memories and details fade from our memories.

Saddest of all, we forget how those words made us feel, which is the most important component. That feeling is key. If we can figure out how to hold on to that feeling, then we are really on to something.

Because, ultimately, they did not plant the seed of greatness within you. They recognized it and helped you bring it to the surface. But it was within you all along, which means it is yours and it belongs to you; it always has and always will. They didn't change you. They revealed you. They revealed you to yourself. That magic is in you. You don't need to be around them constantly to keep feeling that way.

However, if you want that feeling to stay alive, you must be intentional about creating and maintaining that state of being. You have to be intentional about reconnecting with those feelings, surrounding yourself with people who will encourage you and help you see your own light, and developing the skill of reconnecting with those feelings on your own when you don't have the benefit of being around their energy.

Conference Pixie Dust

As I participated in Jack Canfield's Train the Trainer program, I found myself grateful to be in the company of at least 60 people who wanted to change lives in the best possible way. The collective energy of my colleagues was and still is "off-the-charts" amazing. They were the best of the best when it comes to true intentions and service to others: pure, loving souls from all around the world. And when you put all that energy together, something amazing is bound to happen.

In fact, it can be overwhelming if you have never been surrounded by unconditional love and support at that level. It pours over you like the most amazing bath of light, like pure, cosmic, soul-healing energy. When you are in this environment, you become incredibly confident — but instead of being arrogant, you gain confidence that gives you the energy to do things that will help the betterment of others with a very welcoming and warm humility.

When you have the privilege of being in this space, you are humbled because you have been vulnerable. You are humbled because you have been seen for all that you are, with all your imperfections, with all your self-doubt, insecurities, worries, and concerns. All those things that you have tried to forget or overcome have been laid bare -- and even celebrated!

You come to an incredible realization that despite bringing all these things to the light, your compatriots have related to you and fallen in love with you even more because of it. It is unbelievable: you show up in all your imperfections and you work toward a common goal in the presence of people who are committed at the highest level to holding space and lifting others up. Then, in that space, your own beauty and brilliance is shown to you.

With that experience comes the freedom to stand tall, be brave and courageous, and do the things that you admire in others. You realize that your desire means you have the ability to manifest it, whatever it is — otherwise the seed of desire wouldn't have been planted in you.

Make the Feeling Last

But when the training was over, I was left with a big question: how do I make this feeling last? How could I prevent the phenomenon of conference pixie dust from happening to me? I didn't want to feel amazing in the presence of high-vibration people only to have that feeling fade when I was no longer with them. I didn't want the pixie dust to disappear and blow away.

It feels great to learn how to be in a different mode, a mode that makes you feel safer, more supported, and more able to be you. I wanted to maintain this and I wanted to learn to operate in a new, more fun, free-spirited, trusting, personal, and vulnerable way because even though it felt a little foreign, these newfound feelings were worth it.

It was such an emotional experience to leave this environment. On my journey back home, I walked through the Phoenix airport with my heart wide open but no one to respond to it. I was half-expecting people to run up to me and hug me like the people in my training session, but they didn't. It's only natural that when we have a transformational experience with amazing people outside of our normal daily life, we'll have some feelings of confusion and sadness about going back to "the real world."

When you leave, it becomes your responsibility to ensure that the feelings live on and that what they helped you sprout or reveal stays in the light and doesn't get pushed back into the depths of your being, never to be seen again.

The people who bring out the magic in you have shown you what is possible, and that is enough. Even if it was just a glimpse, just a sliver of a peek, that is all the proof you need that what they recognized in you is indeed there. They have also given you clues about how to create this for yourself.

EXERCISE: MEMORIZING THE MAGIC

You owe it to yourself to take advantage of what others have helped you see about yourself. Here are some techniques to keep the memory about what you've learned alive.

Bring to mind someone who makes you feel amazing and inspires you to believe in yourself. Write about how this person made you feel during your interactions with them. This will help you keep the thoughts, feelings, and sensations that were triggered "top of mind" for you. Write in as much detail, including what you felt emotionally and physically in your body. Describe what they said but also perhaps what was communicated without words. What did they say to you with their body language, with the intensity or softness of their voice or with their eyes and energy? What did this experience make you believe about yourself? What did it make you believe about what is or was possible for you?

What was it about them and what they said that made the most profound impact?

What made it possible? Did they make you feel safe to drop your self-consciousness? Did they ask you the right questions about your past accomplishments that allowed you to acknowledge yourself? Did they help you get still enough and quiet enough to admit the truth? Did they help you see something in a new way?

Write a letter to this person expressing your thanks and gratitude and letting them know what they showed you, taught you, and allowed you to feel or realize. This is for you, but if you feel compelled to give it to the person, feel free to do that.

Imagine that you are this person who inspires you to believe in yourself. Write a letter to yourself from them. Express all the things that they communicated to you, even if it wasn't in words. Elaborate and share anything else that wasn't said during the actual interaction, including things that would make you feel even more special and confident if they said them to you. This will help you recognize what you need to know about yourself to grow and move forward.

Return to your vivid description of what the interaction with this person made you feel from Step #2 and read it through, slowly, letting all the words, images, and sensations sink in. Read through it again, periodically closing your eyes to let it sink into your conscious and subconscious bodies. This creates a magical kind of muscle memory that will help you to "turn on" this feeling whenever you want.

Practice recalling this feeling in all of its exquisite detail by closing your eyes and calling up all the feelings, emotions, sensations, and thoughts that bring you back to the magic.

Open your eyes and practice maintaining the feeling of the magic while you're fully awake, aware, and going about your business and fabulousness in the real world.

Repeat. Enjoy. Repeat. Enjoy.

You'll get better at being able to sustain the "feel good" feelings in the absence of the people who make you feel most alive and inspired. When they're available to you, use them: stay in connection and ask for guidance, feedback, and help when you want it.

> *When they're unavailable, don't panic. There are hundreds of thousands of people who can help you see your brilliance. Once you are sure they are out there, you will be able to find them, and they will be able to find you.*

Fake It Like You Mean It

I used to think that faking it was a bad thing. I cringed when people said, "Fake it until you make it." It seemed, well, fake. I felt that if I followed this advice, I would be a fraud. But I learned that, sometimes, faking it can pull things out that you never knew you had in you. At first, it may be hard to make yourself embody characteristics and attributes you want to exude, but once you get into it, acting the part becomes very pleasurable. You begin to experience more freedom to let loose and express yourself in new ways that you normally wouldn't.

Faking it works as a temporary tool, but, ultimately, it doesn't create magic, **unless** it's the kind of simulation that is turbocharged by active creative visualization. If you're going to fake it, you'd better be the best ever at faking this thing. Once you do a knock-out-bang-up job of faking it, guess what? If you're able to do that, it wasn't really faking it. You pulled it from yourself, even if you had to trick yourself into it. You were just doing an exercise in operating at 100% of your capacity.

Faking it works with characteristics and attributes, but it works just as well with embodying certain types of energy, too. It only works well if you are really committed and don't give a half-hearted performance. You have to be all in. Faking it even works when it comes to faking orgasms — sometimes, pretending elicits the real deal. There have been a few times when I gave such a convincing performance of an orgasm that I actually started feeling really good. It was like I was tricking my own body. I started enjoying it so much that I no longer wanted to fake it, so I toned down the show to make the interaction last longer! Your body, mind, and energy will respond to the energy you produce when you put all your energy into "faking it."

EXERCISE: TURNING YOURSELF ON WITH YOUR MIND

Imagine that you are sitting in your own personal movie viewing room. There is a large screen in front of you.

Recall a time when you felt especially sensual, sexual, or turned on.

Picture the scene as vividly as you can. If you can't think of a time when you felt sensually alive, begin to construct your wildest fantasy.

Where are you?

Is anyone with you?

Who is it?

What sounds do you hear? Is there music playing?

Are you indoors or outdoors?

Are there any particular scents you're picking up?

What time of day or night is it?

What are the lighting conditions?

Are you sitting, standing, lying down? What is the surface you are on?

What sort of textures, fabrics, or colors are in the space or room?

Close your eyes and see and feel this in as much detail as you can. Take your time and be very thorough.

Now, pay particular attention to the physical sensations that thinking about this scene produces.

Close your eyes once again and go through and re-experience the feelings you felt as you watch the screen.

> *Notice what sensations come up for you. Start to memorize these feelings. Create the muscle memory for what it feels like to be fully engaged and alive. If you felt a feeling once before, you can absolutely revisit those feelings if you are able to filter out distractions, quiet the mind, and use your imagination to not only mentally remember the times but to relive the visceral experience.*

We often wish that we could re-live happy or fulfilling times. The good news is that you can! The biggest mistake we make is that we intellectualize the experience, thinking of ways that we can make it happen again, brainstorming how to recreate those feelings. This strategy is flawed because it has too much thinking going on. You can't think your way into a feeling; you have to feel your way into a feeling. Use your muscle memory and instincts, creativity, and bodily responses to feel as if you are really there all over again.

EXERCISE: GOLD MEDAL VICTORY POSE

There is one universal posture that most people exhibit when they experience victory or triumph, regardless of what part of the world they live in, what culture they belong to, what religion they practice, or even if they are blind or have never seen someone celebrate this way. They raise their arms above their heads, creating a V shape and sometimes this response is also accompanied by a verbal celebration. Feelings of exhilaration, happiness, and pride create this physical response, which is also typically accompanied by feelings of euphoria and excitement.

Imagine that you have just won a gold medal.

Pretend that you must give an award-winning performance to convince people you have really won that gold medal; throw your hands up in the air, with both fists closed tight

> *and celebrate your victory using your face and your body. Hold that pose for about 10 seconds, taking note of the sensations you feel in your body as you do this.*
>
> *Now, slowly lower your arms by your sides, but see if you can maintain the same feelings in your body as when you had them raised up in glory.*

You can train yourself to feel more alive and full of exhilaration using your thoughts, imagination, memory, and intention.

As you've begun to discover, the wisest, most potent part of you doesn't use words. It uses your body and energy to speak to you. Practice recognizing all the different ways in which your body says "no" and how it says "yes." Consider setting an alert or alarm for every hour you are awake as a reminder to practice flipping the switch and using your senses and energy to turn yourself on, for at least one minute. The more in tune you are with your life-force energy, the more deeply you'll benefit from the practices in Part Two.

Activating Your Three Main Energy Centers

HARA

Cultivate Your Hot, Primal, Sensual Energy

CHAPTER 4

The Mental Prison

Affirmations are overrated. If you are doing "mindset work," you are still "in your head." No amount of affirmations and positive thinking alone will help you feel better on a long-term basis. I tried YEARS of mindset work and still wasn't as confident, happy, and healthy as I wanted to be.

I thought confidence, experience, opportunities, and outward success would make me feel good. I spent tens of thousands of dollars on personal development and tips and tricks to help me get everything I thought I wanted. My thinking went: if I could develop a positive and productive mindset and learn the best success strategies, then I would have the energy and drive to accomplish everything I had always desired.

Was my mindset work helpful? Yes.

But I had to connect with my body and energy before I experienced deep, lasting changes. Going to the body to initiate "feel good" sensations is easier and faster than trying to talk yourself into feeling good. Fighting with your thoughts and getting frustrated when you feel your affirmations aren't working is like trying to run through mud.

Don't get me wrong — affirmations aren't bad. I still love them and use them. But to supercharge them and truly change how you feel, they should be "feeling affirmations" — affirmative statements combined with active visualization to get the body involved.

Baptism by Fire

On my first day on the job as a speaker and facilitator for a national leadership and marketing development firm, I co-presented a conference session in Las Vegas, NV. It wasn't until this day that I met my boss in person for the first time; after we shook hands, she said, "This what we like to call baptism by fire, we're just going to throw you right in."

My mind raced as I sat in the audience watching my new boss speak to the room of about 75 CPA professionals, waiting for my time to speak. I rehearsed in my head. I reviewed my notes while simultaneously trying to pay attention to her. I surveyed the room and made mental notes of my surroundings so that I could start to feel "at home" in this hotel ballroom. I was well-prepared and well-rehearsed. I visualized myself standing up at the front of the room, addressing the audience. Until this point, my largest audience had been about 35 people, but it didn't matter. I felt ready. My new boss and mentor made it look easy, so I wasn't too worried.

What I didn't realize was that even though she made it look easy, for me, it was going to be anything but.

A few minutes into my presentation, my mind was chattering non-stop. I'd noticed a man standing in a far-left side of the room with his arms crossed. The voices inside my head were paranoid and making up stories, saying, "He doesn't agree with what you're saying. He doesn't like you. He's bored and restless. You're talking too fast. You're talking too slow. You aren't making sense."

I continued my presentation, my confidence shaken but my composure steady. I was relieved when my first official work assignment was over.

During dinner, my mentor asked me how it went. I told her, "You know how sometimes you feel like you're floating up here outside and above your body? It was like I was watching myself. I wasn't really in my body." She looked confused, as if I were speaking another language. As I got to know her, I realized why: she's a natural-born speaker. She's never struggled with feeling grounded, centered, and fully present and confident when speaking in front of a group.

By the way, remember that man with crossed arms at the back of the room? During lunch, he introduced himself and thanked me for what I shared. "I really enjoyed it! There was an air conditioning unit right above my head, so I had to stand up and move so I could hear better because I didn't want to miss a word."

As he walked away, I felt amused by my assumptions. By making up negative stories, I'd stolen my ability to be present with my audience. When you can't escape your mental prison, that little negative voice gets stronger, driving us to distraction and obsessive, unconstructive, disempowering thinking.

After that first presentation, I thought I could only go up. I was wrong. It got a lot harder before it got easier.

Number One Fear

Public speaking is often cited as being the number one fear that people have. Public speaking is a perfect example of the dynamic between breath, the mind, and the body. It usually triggers our fight-or-flight response and can cause all sorts of physical, emotional, and physiological responses. It is a high-stress situation — all eyes are on you and you start thinking: *What if I forget what I was going to say, what if I trip and fall, what if I faint, what if I throw up, what if they don't like me, what if what if what if?* If we start believing those worries, we increase the probability that it will happen — the thought becomes a real, likely possibility, and that signal gets transmitted to your brain. Your brain believes you and starts to prepare you to fight or flee.

The good news is that you'll probably survive your public-speaking experience. When it's over, you'll sigh with relief that it's over, that you didn't die, that nothing extreme and horrible happened.

But you can do much more than survive. Any opportunity to communicate with others is an opportunity to connect on a deep level. The number one thing that gets in the way of deep connections, inspiration, and understanding is being in your head instead of being fully present in your interactions. This book is dedicated to helping you connect with your body and your own energy in a way that will make you feel at home wherever you are while simultaneously making you more attractive and intriguing. We will use your senses, the power of your mind, the power of your three energy centers, the power of focus, and your ability to control your breath.

Deep Breaths Are Like Little Love Notes to Your Body

Before I learned proper breath control, when I would stand up to speak in front of even a small group of people, I would immediately feel a little short of breath. It was very difficult to speak in a strong, confident voice when that voice sounded breathy, shaky, and weak.

Shallow, sped-up breathing is one of the first ways we get disconnected from our bodies and start to concentrate all of our energies in our top halves.

Cared-for babies are happy because babies don't spend a lot of time in their heads. They are in tune with what they want, need, and desire, and they are not shy about letting us know. They cry and if we don't listen, they scream. They're persistent; they don't give up easily. They could cry and cry for hours to communicate a need.

Babies also know how to be in the present moment. They know how to breathe. They don't breathe in short breaths, they breathe in long, oxygenating breaths; we can see this if we watch a baby sleep. If you look closely, you see that the baby's tummy moves up and down or in and out. In contrast, most adults breathe in short, shallow breaths into the chest only. Being unsettled and impatient develops this habit. We think that in order to be productive and make a difference, we should move fast and quickly, including breathing shallowly and quickly, and that this will bring with it a sense of accomplishment ... but at what cost? We adversely affect our nervous systems every time we send our bodies into an energy-system frenzy, which happens when we don't breathe properly.

There is a reason that when someone is angry or upset, people tell them to take a deep breath. Deep breaths are proven to calm the nervous system. As an anonymous author said, "Deep breaths are like little love notes to your body."

But many of us don't even know what a true deep breath should look and feel like. It may seem ridiculous that we should have to learn something so simple as breathing: everyone can breathe, right? Technically, yes, everyone can breathe enough to "get by" and stay alive, but let's not be content with simply staying alive — let's treat our bodies as high-performance machines. Your body is the vehicle you use to go out and perform amazing feats. In order for you to do this, your high-performance machine must be in optimal shape. Deep breathing is part of your fueling system. When under conditions of stress, it also tends to be the first thing we lose control of.

Understanding how to use your breath to calm your nervous system is one of the most important and valuable skills you can learn. Breathing is a foundational practice in martial arts, yoga, meditation, and methods designed to help you get out of your head and back into your body.

Some people tell you to "just breathe," as if it were that easy. Before I began my embodiment practices, that advice, to "just breathe" never really helped me. I found the same to be true for the advice, "Connect with your body." For those of us who haven't had an opportunity to explore and discover our bodies and our energy, this feels as simple as the directive "Flap your arms and fly."

Here's one way to start that takes just a few minutes:

EXERCISE: SENSE YOUR BODY TEMPERATURE

Begin by sitting comfortably and gently closing your eyes.

Begin to breathe naturally and comfortably, not worrying about forcing any exaggerated inhalations or exhalations.

Focus on the feeling of the air entering and exiting through your nostrils and/or your mouth.

Imagine that all tension and stress are draining out of your body through your fingers and toes.

Now, begin to focus your attention of the internal temperature of your body. Imagine you are trying to gauge how warm or cold you are throughout your body. Take your time, taking inventory of the internal temperature of the various parts of your body.

Notice where you sense warmth and where you sense coolness. Compare the temperatures of your hands to your feet, for example.

Compare the temperature of your heart center to your lower torso.

Compare one hand to the other. Stay in this exercise for at least two minutes.

You can use a timer to set the time, so you can relax and focus on your body until the alarm goes off.

Next, take a short break, then close your eyes again and continue this practice but this time, start to use your focus and attention to specifically sense the temperature of the palms of each of your hands.

Now, see if you can use your focus and attention to increase the temperature inside your left palm, paying attention to the warmth that is present.

Compare the degree of warmth in your left palm to the level of warmth in your right hand.

Take the last 30 seconds before you open your eyes to notice any changes in your breath rate, relaxation level, and emotional and mental state. With practice, you will deepen your connection with your body and increase your ability to calm your nervous system and become more present.

Breathing Can Be Exhilarating

Just as parents find creative ways to get their kids to eat their vegetables, we can find ways to make breathing fun. Breathing might not seem like the most thrilling activity on the planet; it's easily taken for granted. But it is vital, and when used properly can aid you in strengthening your physical and energetic body, your immune system, magnetism, sensuality, and physical body connection.

EXERCISE: SEXY DARTH VADER BREATH

Begin by finding a comfortable spot in which to relax and start to slow the rate of your breath, breathing deeply and slowly. I've adapted this breathing exercise from one that I learned from my Tantra teacher, Psalm Isadora.

Take the forefinger and middle finger of one hand and slowly and gently bring them to the base of your throat, placing them in that little indentation between your collarbones (clavicles). This area of the body has heightened sensation; gently stimulating this area is a great way to begin to release distracting thoughts.

Begin breathing solely in and out through your nose, concentrating on the sound that you hear while simultaneously feeling and enjoying the vibration you can feel with your fingers at the base of your throat, in that little indentation between your collarbones. If your breath is not audible, begin taking slower, deeper breaths with your mouth closed. (My Tantra teacher used to refer to this sound as a "Sexy Darth Vader" sound.)

See if you can enjoy the sensation of feeling and hearing your breath while gently stimulating this erogenous zone of your body, which will enhance your ability to enjoy this exercise rather than viewing it as something you're supposed to do. The more pleasurable you can make your breathing practice, the more likely you are to do it.

As you continue to breathe deeply in and out through your nose, let your fingers begin to explore away from the base of your neck. Start to caress the skin around your neck and chest. Take your time to enjoy your breath, sound, and touch.

Then, allow your fingers and hands to extend this feather-light touch to your arms, starting with your outer arms and working your way to your inner arms as you continue breathing audibly.

Begin to allow your breath to travel deeper into your body so that you can envision and feel the air — not just coming in and out of your nose, throat, and lungs, but also in and out all the way down to your pleasure power center, a spot located in the approximate center of your pelvic region. For women, it is approximately two-and-a-half to three inches below the navel and for men, it is about two inches below the

> *navel. Take a moment to visualize where this place is within your body. Envision your inhaled breaths going down and deep enough in your body so that they reach your pleasure power center.*
>
> *To further enhance your ability to send breath to your pleasure power center, imagine that there is a tube extending from your neck to the base of your spine, through the center of your body. As you inhale and exhale, send the breath and vital life-force energy up and down through this tube. Take deep and complete breaths, so you can send air all the way to the bottom and all the way back up to the top.*
>
> *Continue this practice for a few minutes. Notice how much calmer your nervous system becomes and how much more present you are.*

Managing Your Mental Chatter

As you get ready to connect to your pleasure power center on a deeper level, it is helpful to clear your mind of distracting and worrisome thoughts. First, take a few moments to simply notice what you are experiencing on a mental, emotional, and physical level. Taking just three minutes, close your eyes and first notice any physical sensations, pains, tightness, areas of tension, and areas where you feel particularly strong, flexible or open. Then, take another minute to notice the different kinds of emotions that may be swirling around. Finally, take the last minute to watch your thoughts, taking note of your mental state.

Then, begin dissociating from your thoughts, emotions, and any physical symptoms, which are our most frequent distractions as human beings.

For example, if I am angry and frustrated that my colleague has not replied to my message, I would focus on dissociating from my thoughts and feelings about the situation. I might repeat the phrase, "I have the thought that Mark should have responded to me by now." There is a big energetic difference between saying, "Mark should have replied to me by now" and "I have the thought that Mark should have replied to me by now." Try saying those two sentences out loud and feel the difference.

Similarly, if I am angry that the bank rejected my application for a business loan, instead of focusing on my anger and disappointment, I would repeat the phrase, "I have anger, I am not my anger," as I focus on breathing from my power center. "I have feelings of disappointment, I am not my disappointment." With every breath, I connect deeper to the part of me that can absorb and transform anger and disappointment into something useful and of a higher vibration.

This helps to clear the slate, freeing your mind and emotional and energetic body to benefit the most from your power center connection practice.

Alternatively, you can use a simple mantra such as one of the following:

My body is not me, but mine. My mind is not me, but mine. My emotions are not me, but mine.

I have a body, I am not my body. I have thoughts, I am not my thoughts. I have emotions, I am not my emotions.

You can practice reciting these statements, or your own customized statements, as you focus your attention on your pleasure power center.

Many times, I prefer to clear my mind during my power center connection exercise, but at other times, I will process using another favorite exercise I learned from Rick Carson, author of *Taming Your Gremlin*. Carson refers to our little negative voices as Gremlins; he recommends turning your little negative voices into characters so that you can more easily recognize them when they pop up and be less likely to buy into what they're saying and let them take over.

When I took myself through the "Taming Your Gremlin" process, I created a character named "Little Miss Worry Wart."

I drew her with a big head because she's always thinking: her only activity is to come up with worst-case scenarios 24/7. She thinks she's so smart, so I drew her with glasses. I drew a couple of dialogue boxes coming out of her mouth saying things like, "Oh, no, what if I make a fool of myself?" "What if this cold turns into pneumonia?" or "What if our plane crashes on the way to New York?"

Assigning these voices to characters help me stay aware of the fact that these voices are not me. I don't have to fall into the trap of believing what they tell me — I can deal with my internal dialogue in an objective, and sometimes amused, manner.

These little negative voices are often present when we feel fearful, confused, disappointed, overwhelmed, or self-critical.

EXERCISE: TAME YOUR GREMLIN

Think of a time in the recent past that you experienced an overwhelming, fearful, confused, disappointed, or nervous response. Close your eyes and put yourself back into that state of mind. What thoughts were going through your head? When you open your eyes, immediately take out a sheet of paper and write all the thoughts that were going through your mind. Then, draw a character for one of your little negative voices that tends to rear its ugly head and feed you negative or disempowering thoughts.

One of the things that makes my little negative voices scream is when I'm dealing with a health crisis. We all have a hard-wired instinct to survive; when our life or health is threatened, our systems can react powerfully, even if it's not helpful. I'm one of those people who should never search a health symptom online, because if I'm not mindful of those voices in my head, the search results could convince me that I have a deadly disease. When I got a huge, infected bite from an unknown creature in the woods of Minneapolis, the information I gathered from the internet and from the doctors fed Little Miss Worry Wart just the information she needed to tell me, "Your blood stream is probably infected and you might have Lyme Disease."

And when I experienced a lengthy, scary bout of unexplained dizziness, those voices really started to roar.

Symptoms Are Warning Signals

My husband, Brian, and I had ordered chicken salad from our favorite Scottsdale restaurant and were enjoying it at our makeshift dining room table — the desk in our hotel room. About halfway through the meal, I started to feel dizzy and light-headed. It was August in Arizona, so I thought maybe I was dehydrated. But even after a meal and a full glass of water, when I stood up to try to reorient myself, I felt even worse. I tried to relax, but by the end of the evening, I needed to hold onto the walls to make my way to the bathroom. The room spun and the lights made me squint as I looked in the mirror. I tried to lie down, hoping that would help, but as I looked up at the ceiling, the room continued to spin.

My brain raced: was it something I ate? What could have triggered this dizziness, and what did I need to do to make it stop? But the more I thought about, the more nervous and fearful I got. I wanted to enjoy the rest of our weekend and I had a lot of work to do when I got back home.

By the time we got home, the dizziness had worsened. Panic set in — in seven days, I was delivering two keynote presentation to more than 300 women at a conference in Philadelphia, and I needed the week to rehearse.

But over the next week, the symptoms continued to worsen and the triggers for my dizziness began to multiply. Noise, movement, light, walking on uneven surfaces, repetitive motions among countless other things made me dizzy.

I was so dizzy I could barely leave my house, and when I did it was only for less than an hour at a time. Out in the world, everything affected me. I couldn't drive — my husband, mom, or dad had to drive me everywhere — and even when I was a passenger, the moving cars on the road made me increasingly unsteady. Power lines hanging in the air swayed, nauseating me. Car lights, street lights, any light attacked my nervous system. I couldn't listen to music with words or any loud music because my system could not take in the sound stimulation without an awful spinning sensation.

At home, I could barely complete simple repetitive movements like moving my toothbrush back and forth. I had a hard time taking a shower; tilting my head back even slightly to rinse my hair knocked me off kilter. I had to focus very hard to keep my balance because my feet could feel the slightly uneven tiles on the shower floor. Every small task felt like a major undertaking. I had to rest after taking a shower. Eating breakfast in sight of the swaying windchime hanging outside our breakfast nook made me feel sick. Any television program with loud sounds or rapid movements was off-limits.

I didn't have time to be off balance. I needed every spare second to work, rehearse, and prepare for the upcoming presentation. I tried to do a complete dress rehearsal of my presentation, but my high heels felt precarious, so I practiced barefoot and tried not to think about wearing them for the real, live presentation.

I went to urgent care, where they referred me to an ear, nose, and throat doctor whose next available appointment was in three weeks.

This speaking engagement had been on the calendar for a year; I couldn't back out of it. They were expecting me, and I felt obligated to honor my commitment to serve as their keynote speaker.

With no answers, and no relief in sight, I had no choice but to fly to Philadelphia in the worst condition of my life.

CHAPTER 5

Pleasure Power Center

I sat in the low vinyl seat at the airport gate, laptop open, crying, and pretending to work. I tried to wipe away the first few tears and preserve my makeup, but I couldn't keep up, so I just let them fall, mascara running down my cheeks. People nearby stared at me, likely wondering if someone had died, or I'd just said goodbye to a loved one, or I'd just lost my job?

My equilibrium was still spinning, yet in 48 hours, I'd be giving two separate 90-minute keynote presentations for some 300 hundred women. This was the first time I'd left the house alone in the week since I'd fallen ill with this mysterious dizziness. My body was still extremely sensitive to light, sound, movement, and all kinds of stimulation. I was terrified that boarding the plane would exacerbate my vertigo, trapping me in an inescapable small space with my senses misfiring.

The night before, I'd been swallowed whole by my very first anxiety attack. I sat in the passenger seat of the car as my husband helped me run a final errand. My mind raced: how would I be able to speak on stage for three hours when I couldn't drive or sleep lying down without getting dizzy? How would I survive the flight? A cab would take me to the hotel and the venue, which provided some comfort and reassurance. I'd had to rehearse barefoot — would my usual high heels make me so dizzy that I'd fall onstage?

Suddenly, my husband opened the driver side door. The abrupt noise and movement startled me so badly that an acid wave of rage at my husband broke over my body, for giving me no warning. Chills and goosebumps prickled over my left shoulder with an intensity I'd never felt.

Six hours later, that startled sensation still hadn't gone away. My shoulder still tingled, unnerving me. I sat on my bedroom floor, the place I instinctively went when I felt so light-headed. I bawled, watching my husband and daughter playing outside, wishing I could call out and ask for someone to be with me, to hold me, but I didn't want to scare my daughter. So, I stayed inside, letting the tears flow, doing what I could to console myself.

As I prepared for takeoff, I prayed that I wouldn't experience any sudden, scary symptoms as we climbed to our cruising altitude, because I had been told that my condition could be related to an inner-ear issue and the airplane pressure changes could affect me. I was relieved when the pilot announced he was turning off the seatbelt sign and we were free to move about the cabin. I had made it through the riskiest part of the flight.

Usually I reviewed and rehearsed during a flight, but this time I needed to do something more important. I turned to the special meditation I had been using to calm my system and ground myself when the world was spinning: The Art of Feminine Presence™ meditation. I listened to the songs that were played while I learned this practice from my teacher and mentor, the same music that played as we practiced during the teacher training. Just hearing the first few bars of a song transported me back to that place where I felt a deep connection to my divine feminine source of energy. The music soothed my soul and the meditation practice grounded me in my body.

I had prayed for mastery, and this was my chance to develop and demonstrate it. In my marketing materials, presentations, and social media posts, I had been telling people they could feel grounded and confident no matter what came their way. This illness was testing my beliefs. I had to trust the processes and practices: this time, it wasn't about feeling motivated, sexy, confident, or magnetic just for fun. This time my reputation was on the line. I was about to find out if the practices I'd been touting were powerful enough to help me feel calm and centered in the middle of a physical storm.

I practiced this meditation for the entire two legs of my flight, more than five hours combined. When I arrived safely at my hotel room, I briefly considered rehearsing my presentation, but after a few minutes, I returned to my meditation because I knew it was the only thing that would save me. In the morning, instead of jumping into action, I calmly stayed in bed for a few minutes and allowed my body and entire system to ease into consciousness while repeating positive affirmations. I moved slowly and mindfully as I got ready for the day. I knew that if I moved about in a rushed pace my energy would become frantic.

I didn't know if this strategy was going to pay off, but I had trust and faith that it would. And it did. It worked. Plus, the Universe seemed to be on my side. When I entered the venue, calm spread through me as I saw the unusual stage setup — sunken lecture-style instead of raised. I'd known that I was going to Penn State University but I hadn't considered the possibility that I'd be speaking in a lecture hall. This whole time, I was picturing speaking on a raised stage.

But thankfully, I was wrong; instead I'd be looking up at the audience, which made it much less likely that I'd experience dizziness from looking down.

I survived the presentations. Pleased that they'd gone well and glad they were over, I took a cab straight from the venue to the airport; the driver's music seemed to be blaring unbearably loudly, but I said nothing, unsure if it was really that loud. I moved through the airport at a slow, steady pace to stay calm and prevent my heart rate and anxiety from creeping up. I was amazed that I had pulled it off and grateful for the opportunity, but anxious to get home and stay in my house to try to shield myself from all the stimuli that felt like an assault on my senses.

Although it helped to be home, there were still triggers everywhere: the buzz of the microwave timer, doors closing, ice clanking into a glass. My instincts often sent me to the floor to find a sense of grounding. I would hold weighty rocks and gemstone crystals to make me feel heavier and less likely to spin off into the air with my unsteadiness. I slept beneath pillows, rocks and heavy gemstones to make me feel grounded. Sleeping was no longer a peaceful experience. As much as I longed to close my eyes and rest, the simple act of closing my eyes would trigger the spinning sensation. Lying down with my eyes closed made things even worse, so I had to sleep sitting up for more than four months.

I had to stop and listen. My body was trying to tell me to slow down and pay attention. I couldn't do anything, really, so my only job was to figure out how to get better, which involved getting to know my body better. I had to become best friends with my physical self, my emotional self, and my energetic field. I had to develop the skill of noticing when something was "off" energetically, when a feeling, an emotion or a person was triggering a stress response. I had to become acutely aware of all my triggers, reactions, and the interconnectedness between the various systems in my body — most specifically, my nervous system, which was in total havoc.

I wondered if the doctors or anybody would ever figure out what was wrong with me. The ear, nose, and throat doctor checked to make sure that tiny calcium carbonate crystals hadn't gotten loose in my ear canal and tried to perform a technique called the Eppley Maneuver. It didn't work. He diagnosed my condition as non-vestibular dizziness, or vertigo, and said there was nothing we could do except wait. For most people, symptoms resolved themselves within six weeks.

It seemed like an eternity to just wait and wonder. But I had no other choice. After six weeks, the symptoms were not only present, but they'd gotten worse. The doctors still could not identify a medical cause for my condition. Eventually, after many visits to various specialist and practitioners, I saw a brain specialist. After many tests and thousands of dollars spent out of pocket, I felt no better and walked away with a new diagnosis of "chronic non-vertiginous dizziness" — which basically meant, "It's not vertigo, but you're dizzy, and we have no idea why or how to help you."

Send Me A Sign

Somehow, I managed to continue working through the illness, even if at a much-reduced pace. Nine months later, after delivering a talk at a women's networking group where I was leading a session on confidence and pleasure power centers, a Korean woman named Hongik came up to me and said, "I know what you're talking about. That place in the center point of gravity in our bodies that you were teaching us to connect to, it's called 'Lower Dantien' in Korea, and in our version of yogic practice, we call it 'Dahn-jon.'" She and I connected over our mutual interest in how to make contact both physically and energetically with this place in the body. As we spoke, my intuition spoke within me — not a little voice in my head, but a force that made me speak up and move, almost involuntarily. Three separate times, as she walked away, I walked toward her, asking another question or finding another way to keep the conversation going.

Eventually, I mentioned my ongoing dizziness; Hongik told me she had a former client with a similar condition who had benefitted tremendously from healing energetic sessions with her. I booked an appointment with her right then and there. Two days later, as she did healing work on me during a private session, I told her that even my "alternative" doctors were recommending that I consider a CAT scan or MRI to rule out a brain condition or disorder.

After evaluating me, she said, "No, you don't need that. You're okay. We just need to figure out how to bring all of the heat and energy that is in your head back down." She did some healing work on me and then she taught me three exercises to do at least twice per day, 15 minutes each session. I started doing them that day and was religious about doing them every morning and every night.

Within about five days, I felt about 90 percent better.

As a result of spending the majority of my life in my head bubble, I had accumulated a lot of energy in my head. For someone who is a very cerebral person, practicing connecting to your pleasure power center via visualization and meditation by itself can help redirect energy, but for others, this will not be enough. That was the case for me: I needed more active, physical practices to help bring the energy down from my head and into my pleasure power center so I could feel powerfully grounded in my center point of gravity.

During our session, Hongik introduced me to a tool we would use to help me connect to my dahn-jon. It was called a belly button wand. It was yellow and it was the shape of the capital letter "T." When I saw it, I knew I was on the right healing track. In a recent meditation and prayer session, I had asked for a sign to help me understand how to get better.

During the meditation, I had received an image of the letter "T." My first interpretation had been that maybe it had something to do with my thyroid gland, but I had been staying open to the possibilities. When I saw that yellow T-shaped contraption, I knew I was on the right track.

Some of the techniques that I'm going to share with you in this book are based on or adapted from exercises that I picked up from Master Hongik, and some are based on or a blend of what I've learned from my Tantra teacher, my Art of Feminine Presence teacher and my embodiment and speaking coaches.

I was shocked and amazed at how quickly and effectively physical and energetic practices could help me shift my physical condition as well as my mental and emotional conditions. The exercises are fairly simple to do, they don't take an enormous amount of time to complete, they produce quick results, and they feel good, so they don't feel like work or like something that you "have to do."

Even though some of my friends and family might have thought them strange, I did my energetic and grounding practices consistently, because they worked! Through continuous and consistent practice, I have been able to manage stress, overwhelm, and overthinking. Sometimes, feelings of dizziness, lightheadedness, neck tension, eye fatigue, or headaches may occur, especially if I am spending a lot of time in large groups or crowded places, but if this happens, I now have a collection of healing and meditation practices I can use to return to a balanced emotional, energetic, and mental state.

Escape The Mental Prison

Many of us have the problem of spending too much time "in our heads." Modern lifestyles and its issues and concerns make people prone to worry, overthinking, overanalyzing, and obsessing. This mental emphasis can invert the ideal energy balance in the body. Traditional Chinese medicine describes a condition known as Water Up, Fire Down as ideal. Water Up, Fire Down means that you have a cool, clear head and hot, fiery energy in the lower part of your torso where the digestive and reproductive systems live. But when people get stuck in their heads, they begin to develop too much energy and heat in the head and too little in their body's "power center." A lack of heat and energy flow in your power center often results in digestive issues, lack of drive, energy, stamina, sex drive, "mojo," and motivation. When you don't have the "fire in your belly," you don't have the energy and determination to make things happen.

When you are "in your head," your energy and attention are actually not really in your physical head. Your energy and attention are actually outside of your body, usually in the space right above and off to the side of your head like a little cartoon bubble where your thoughts scroll like dialogue. When we think too much, and our focus is on our thoughts, we become dissociated from our bodies.

We all have cool, water energy and hot, fire energy running through our bodies. Ideally, cool water energy will travel up to your head and keep it cool while the hot fire energy rests in your pelvic region. But sometimes, the balance and orientation of these energies gets flipped.

People who are easily angered and upset are often called "hot heads." This is because when our emotional state gets flustered, heat rises to our heads. In this upside-down energetic state, when there is cool energy in your dahn-jon as opposed to heat, you may experience symptoms like poor digestion or low sex drive.

Many of the exercises in this section of the book will help you to create the proper balance by generating heat in your pleasure power center and keeping your head cool.

Anger isn't the only sign that you've accumulated too much heat in your upper energy center. Simply having too many busy thoughts, even if they are neutral, can negatively impact your energy balance. People who think too much, in general, will benefit from learning to cultivate more energy in the pleasure power center to restore your body to their optimal water up, fire down state.

Let's practice consciously bringing your attention and energy back to your body every time you catch yourself being stuck in your head bubble. Connecting with your pleasure power center will help you get in the habit of taking at least a few moments to bring your energy body back to you by putting your attention on your physical being, on your breath, and the sensation of what it feels like to have your energy body back inside of you.

Meet Your Pleasure Power Center

Your pleasure power center is located in the center of your body approximately 2 ½ to 3 inches below your navel and about two inches inside your body. This is the area of your body where your "life-force energy" or "mojo" lives, also referred to as "qi energy" or "chi energy" (different spellings with the same pronunciation).

Connecting to this energetic space within your body is the most foundational aspect of this work. You have a physical body — your bones, muscles, blood, tendons, etc. — and then you have an energetic body, which consists of the life-force energy that runs through and around your body.

Your pleasure power center is the magical place within your physical and energetic body where your drive, stamina, and creativity are sourced, and it is where you can tap into to feel more productive, sexier, more present, in touch with your inner wisdom and centered and grounded, since it is literally your center point of gravity.

Your pleasure power center stores heat and energy; physical strength and stamina originate from there. It is also considered to be the "house" of communications, sensory awareness, and feelings. When something is going on in your environment or in another person, you can sometimes feel it before you can recognize it mentally — we often call it a "gut feeling."

Your gut is also known as your "second brain" because it can function independently without help from your brain. The gut brain has its own nervous system, called the enteric nervous system, and is equipped with its own senses and reflexes. Over 90 percent of your serotonin (the "feel good" hormone) is produced by your gut, which helps explain why much of our emotional state is tightly connected with our gut. For example, this is why you may experience "butterflies" in your stomach when you get nervous and when people describe getting sick to their stomachs upon hearing bad news.

Your gut brain lives in the same area as your intuition. The sensations can be subtle, but the more you practice connecting there, the more in tune you will be with what your "second brain" is trying to tell you.

Connecting to this energetic space within your body is common across many different practices and traditions, some of which are centuries old. Most martial artists, Zen practitioners, and yogis call it the "Dantien." In Chinese QiGong, it is known as the "Lower Dantien." In Korean yoga, it is referred to as "Dahn-jon" and in Japanese traditions, it is called the "Hara," which translates to the word "heat." Sufi traditions refer to this space as "Kath." In The Art of Feminine Presence body of work, we frequently refer to it as "womb space." In this book, I will refer to this energetic center point of gravity as your pleasure power center.

EXERCISE: PLEASURE POWER CENTER CONNECTION

This visualization is best done with your eyes closed; consider recording yourself reading the instructions and then playing it back for yourself with your eyes closed.

Find a comfortable standing, sitting, or lying-down position.

Recall what it feels like to "turn on" and feel sensation in your body. Feel the energy and aliveness that is circulating between your hips, between your belly button, your perineum and the base of your spine. Feel the energy circulating throughout your entire pelvic region.

Imagine that you have a bowl sitting inside of your pelvis. The top rim of the bowl is at about the level of your hips and circles all the way around from hip to hip and from your belly button and all around to the back of your spine and back around to your belly button. Imagine that at the very bottom of this bowl is a spoonful of liquid honey. Feel the honey gently swirling around the base of your pelvic bowl.

This energetic space known as your pelvic bowl contains your sexual organs, gut brain, and your pleasure power center. Your energetic power center is located approximately two-and-a-half to three inches below your navel, suspended in the middle of your pelvic bowl.

Since we are trying to connect to an "invisible" spot within your body, it's helpful to use your imagination to visualize an image there. I recommend visualizing a small globe of light suspended in the center of your pelvis. But, you can use any imagery that appeals to you the most: a diamond, stone, lotus flower, flame, heart, or anything else that comes to mind. For example, sometimes I like to envision a diamond that is reddish-pink or sometimes a white lotus flower or black sphere. It depends on my mood — you can choose whatever serves you best in the moment. It doesn't need to make logical sense: if it feels right, it's right for you.

You can imagine that in that space there exists a small, suspended sphere of light, made up of brilliant light energy. Imagine that this sphere of light is living and breathing with you, inside of you. As you inhale, it expands, and as you exhale, it contracts back to its original size. Spend at least one full minute focusing on the expansion and contraction of this sphere of light suspended in your pelvic region.

Connecting with this space as a meditation practice with your eyes closed will help you deepen your connection to your body and to this space and offer a relaxation response that provides a sense of internal strength.

Although it is easier for most people to connect with their power centers with their eyes closed, ideally we also want to get good at doing it with our eyes open, as we go about our days and as we interact with people. The next exercise will help you learn to hold attention on your pleasure power center as you interact with people so that you can remain centered and create better connection during conversations.

EXERCISE: HEAD BUBBLE

Start to worry about something. Allow yourself a few moments of obsessive worry. Notice what happens to your body and energy. Notice where your energy goes.

For most people, this is similar to what it feels like when you are "in your head." Your mind starts racing and your body starts reacting in a nervous or otherwise unfavorable way.

Now, imagine that you are about to introduce yourself to a group of people. Nervous energy runs through your body and a million thoughts run through your head. "What will I say?" "Will I sound smart?" "Will they like me?" "Do I have food stuck in my teeth?" "Is my zipper zipped up or not?"

It is useful to cultivate this feeling on purpose so that you can notice what it's like to be stuck in your head bubble. Different people experience different signs and symptoms, but you may experience some of the following:

- *Rapid heart rate*
- *Sweating*
- *Nervous habits like playing with your keys or the change in your pocket as you talk*
- *Looking up at the ceiling or feeling as if you are looking up into space and not maintaining eye contact*
- *Speaking very quickly*
- *Speaking very slowly*
- *Speaking in a high-pitched voice*
- *Speaking in a monotone voice*
- *Being too serious*
- *Rambling*

Once you've put yourself into this head bubble state, practice introducing yourself to this imaginary group of people. Pay attention to how you feel and how you sound.

Then, go through the pleasure power connection exercise above before trying your introduction again, but this time staying connected to the center point of your pelvis as you speak.

When I discuss this concept in a workshop, I will typically do a demonstration. I will purposely put myself into my head bubble so that people can experience what I am like in that state. I ask them to take a mental snapshot of that version of me.

Then, for contrast, I leave my head bubble and connect with my pleasure power center and introduce myself from there. Again, I ask them to take a snapshot of that version of me.

Then, I ask for feedback. This is what I tend to hear about Head Bubble Michelle versus Pleasure Power Center Michelle:

- *Head bubble Michelle sounded a little bit fake and rehearsed*
- *Your voice the first time was high-pitched*
- *When you switched into your power center, your voice was more resonant*
- *You spoke a lot faster the first time*
- *The first time sounded like a list of accomplishments or a resume*
- *You shared more personal details when you were connected to your power center*
- *Your body seemed nervous when in your head bubble*
- *The head bubble version seemed to last so much longer (even though I make sure to make both the same length of time)*
- *You seemed more relatable, vulnerable, and human in your power center*
- *You made more eye contact and connected more with us when you were in your power center*
- *I remember more of what you said the second time*

After practicing once by yourself or in the mirror, practice during real conversations with people. Notice the differences in how you feel in each mode and how differently people respond to you.

EXERCISE: TWO EYEBALLS

As you interact with people in the world, practice the two eyeballs exercise I learned from my mentor, Rachael Jayne. It's very simple. Every time you see two eyeballs looking at you, take that as your cue to connect to your power center. This helps you consistently ask yourself if you're in your head or if you're connected to your power center.

Authentic Communication

Once you've started conditioning yourself to connect frequently and as much as possible to your power center, practice talking and listening from your power center.

This sounds a little quirky, but it works. While you are talking, you can imagine that the words are coming from your power center. You may even visualize a mouth connected to your power center that is doing the talking. When you do this, you will notice that your sharing is more genuine and interesting, rather than sharing only the things that your mind thinks you "should" share or that which is "appropriate" or practical.

Use the same concept for listening. Imagine that your power center has ears and as you listen, listen from there. This will help you listen to understand rather than trying to problem-solve as you listen or predicting what they're going to say next, or having your thoughts trail off somewhere else taking you away from what the other person is saying.

Getting the Giggles

At some point during most days of Jack Canfield's Train the Trainer program, Jack would lead us through a guided meditation. One of his favorites is a meditation called the Tree of Life Meditation. During that particular meditation, Jack would lead us through a process of connecting with, activating, and delivering life-force energy though eight different sephirot or energy centers of our bodies starting from the top of our heads and down to the soles of our feet. This name for the tree of life energy centers comes from the ancient spiritual tradition of Kabbalah.

After our training one day, one of my fellow trainers laughed with me about how he couldn't help but get the giggles, like a teenage boy, every time Jack spoke about connecting us to the sephirot of "Yesod," which is linked to the pelvic region and is where we have the power to create life. We laughed, but it wasn't until years later that I realized how important and powerful this sephirot is. It is true that feeling and connecting with it can make us feel giddy. That's part of its appeal. Some people tend to shy away from that energy because it may carry some shame or feel like connecting with it is a guilty pleasure. But learning to fully appreciate it, understanding its power and potency is key to realizing our inner strength power and potential.

Center of Creation

The Universe wants you to use the qi energy in your pleasure power center to create. The Universe doesn't care if you create another human or not, it just wants you to create something, whether it be a project, song, poem, social movement, a new business, an invention, a book, a community ... And if you invest time and effort into cultivating and directing this energy for the sake of creation and improvement of human life in some form, the Universe will reward you by giving you more and more qi energy to create more and to fuel and energize yourself for your efforts.

A Meditation That Feels Like a Guilty Pleasure

Often, people don't meditate at all or enough to receive its benefits because it becomes boring at some point. Most of us have to use willpower to develop the discipline to meditate. This happens even for people who are "good" meditators, and people who have experienced meditation's profound effects. In the most basic sense, humans are motivated by pain and pleasure, and I believe that meditation motivated by acquiring pleasure is much more effective than practices motivated by avoiding pain.

One of the ways to wake up and shake up our life-force energy or mojo is to intentionally feel pleasure in our bodies. This accomplishes a lot at once. Because it feels good, it reduces stress, and releases tension in the body. We also stimulate the parasympathetic nervous system, our body's natural relaxation mechanism.

When you are able to quiet your mind, connect with divine energy, and bring it into your body, you can enter a state of connectedness and the kind of bliss that is unique to meditation. In this place, you feel supported, loved, and enveloped in unconditional love. You are able to be present and free from the overactive mind.

When I discovered the The Art of Feminine Presence meditation practice, I realized that it is a very unique meditation style. It is specifically designed to help cultivate and move feminine energy. Someone who has feminine energy as their dominant energy mode is better suited at times to a type of meditation designed to help them connect specifically with feminine energy. Feminine energy likes to flow; it likes movement and it is excited when the senses are awakened. And one of the best ways to awaken your senses is to use your sexual energy to create pleasurable feelings in your body. Another effective way to connect you with your senses is music. This is also why we typically practice our Art of Feminine Presence meditation with music and with slight movement. I can't explain it in detail here because it can only be taught in person, but I can say it is different from any other type of meditation you have probably experienced, and it is especially effective at helping you wake up, build up, and radiate your powerful, creative, sensual, magnetic feminine energy.

Similarly, meditation practices for men that focus on sensing energy in the power center area can also evoke many pleasurable sensations and feelings. When one practices a form of meditation that circulates throughout the body the life-force energy originating in the power center, meditation begins to feel like a guilty pleasure rather than something we "should" do because it's good for us. When I started meditating this way, I thought it was almost too good to be true!

Tools for Strengthening Your Connection to Your Pleasure Power Center

The strategies we'll use to activate the energy in and around your power center will focus on stimulating or "waking up" three main points in and around your power center:

- Your belly button region

- The center of your pelvic region

- Near the base of your pelvis, more specifically your perineum, anal and pelvic control muscles

Many of us have some numbness or some shame around putting attention on our sexuality, reproductive organs, or on feeling good simply for the purpose of feeling good. Most of us have had some bad experiences; we've been told that is not what "good" girls or boys do, or we may be so used to leading with our brains that we're out of touch with our pleasure center and the wisdom, power, and energy it can generate. Here are some exercises to help you "wake up" your vital life-force energy and begin to activate your pleasure power center.

Pleasure Power Center Warm-Up Exercises

Hip Circles - Start to wake up that life force energy by doing a few hip circles, side to side in each direction (preferably while playing some sensual music).

Hip Thrusts - Once you've done a series of hip circles in each direction, transition into some pelvic thrusts, making sure to keep a slight bend in your knees while you gently thrust your hips forward and backward in the most pleasurable way possible.

Secret Squeezes - Pelvic control muscle squeezes will further awaken the energy in and around your pelvic area and power center. These secret squeezes entail contracting and releasing your pelvic control muscles. These pelvic floor muscles offer support to your pelvic organs, including your urethra, bladder, and bowel. You can locate these muscles and find the right technique by engaging the same motion that you would if you were trying to stop the flow of urine.

A traditional Kegel may be approached as more of a physical exercise with the sole intention of strengthening the muscle, but with our secret squeezes, the intention and focus of energy is what distinguishes them from a purely mechanical exercise. You can multi-task while doing Kegels, but with our secret squeezes, we maintain our focus of attention on the sensation and on the idea of using this exercise as a way to prime the pump — to begin to build up life-force energy and stir up sensation and intensity in our pleasure power center.

This practice is also a meditation practice meant to cleanse and strengthen you physically and energetically while simultaneously calming you, exciting you, and connecting you with your physical body so that you can experience less anxiety, stress, worry, and self-consciousness.

Practice contracting your pelvic floor muscles while enjoying the energy that swirls around your pelvic bowl. As you focus your energy and attention here, tighten your pelvic floor muscles with the intention of strengthening the energy on your first and second power centers while whispering the sound "Ahh." As you enjoy the sensation created by the secret squeeze of your PC muscles, enjoy the release that comes from audibly saying "Ahh," knowing that in doing so, you are releasing tension and negative energy with each breath.

Giddy-Up

Imagine that you are riding a galloping horse and start rocking your pelvis forward and back. Keep your body loose, allowing your head to follow and bob up and down, and allowing your energy to begin to flow more freely in your body.

Power Center Stimulation

When I started practicing Tantra and feminine and masculine energy work, I began by using meditation and visualization to connect with my power center. These practices were valuable, and I still use them, but as I started teaching these techniques to more people, I realized that some people have a difficult time connecting to an energetic space that they can't see or touch. This may occur for a variety of different reasons; many people experience numbness or a lack of sensation in the pelvic region due to sexual trauma or shame, and some people have difficulty with visualization and meditation in general.

Whatever the case, it can be helpful to incorporate physical stimulation of your power center from the outside of your physical body.

You can use your fingers and fists to tap certain parts of your body, similar to some of the energetic practices that are practiced in Qi Gong and Tai Chi.

Either stand with your feet about hip-width apart or get in a comfortable seated position, either cross-legged or in a chair where your feet can be firmly planted on the ground.

Make fists with both of your hands and begin tapping on your lower abdomen with the outsides of your hands (pinky finger side of your hand) about two to two-and-a-half inches below your navel, using alternating fists, in rapid succession, touching your lower abdominal region. Alternate your fists in a rapid fashion and make sure that you continue to breathe.

Don't worry about the exact positioning and placement of your hand. Regardless of your precision, you will still be waking up the energy in and around your power center. In fact, I frequently allow my fists to travel farther up my body between my belly button and chest area, stimulating my solar plexus area after or during this practice to strengthen my will-power, courage, and entire third-chakra energy center, which helps to dissipate any feelings of fear or anxiety.

I recommend doing this for a minimum of five minutes every day. You will notice that you have more energy, more clarity, and enhanced intuition. You'll feel less scattered and worried, and you'll enjoy more sensual, powerful life-force energy.

Shake Your Body or Do Rebounding Exercise

This movement activates your lymphatic system, aiding in digestion and immune functions, gets your blood circulating, releases stagnant energy, and activates your body's natural healing power.

You can choose to shake gently or vigorously as you move or stretch, helping your own energy to circulate and replenish itself. You can start with your hands and arms, or anywhere you like. Start to incorporate your hips, your torso, your legs, shoulders, adding in more body parts to shake. This will begin to open up your energy channels so that the powerful energy you generate in your power center can travel to and heal all parts of your body and energetic system.

Whole body shaking is something that you can do anytime, anywhere, to re-energize and loosen up. I recommend doing this to any kind of rhythmic drumming music. Alternatively, you may wish to use a rebounder, which is a mini trampoline that you can use for the physical, emotional, and energetic benefits of bouncing and shaking.

Buttock Bouncing

Lie on the floor with your back flat, feet flat, and knees bent. Lift up your buttocks so that you form a downward diagonal line with your legs extending from your hips to your feet. Then simply let your buttocks drop to the ground, making a boom noise on the floor. Lift your buttocks back up after a couple of seconds and repeat the dropping and lifting motion repeatedly for between one and five minutes. This motion will send energy to your pelvic region, helping to ground and center you and engage the aliveness of your life force energy as it circulates throughout your power center area, while helping to bring down excess energy from your head.

The Breath of Fire

Breath of Fire is a fundamental yogic practice that helps you connect with your body, release tension, and activate your pleasure power center, which is the storage place for vitality, energy, and overall "mojo." It is also a very effective way of waking up your life-force energy and starting to undo some of the numbing that may have occurred below the belt for a variety of reasons including childbirth, abdominal surgery, C-section, sexual abuse, or sexual shaming. It is done by rapidly pumping the navel point in and out while breathing rapidly only through the nose. As you "suck in" the navel point, you exhale deeply through the nose and then as you release the navel point, you inhale.

Practice this breathing exercise for at least two minutes per day to activate your energetic power and life force. If you start to feel like you need to stop because your core muscles get tired, just keep going! If it feels like you are doing abdominal crunches and you're tempted to stop before the two-minute mark — you're doing it right!

Advanced Practice

Once you've gotten some practice at isolating and contracting and releasing your PC (pelvic control) muscles, experiment with noticing if you are also contracting your anus at the same time when you practice. If so, see if you can isolate the PC muscles by trying to contract only those muscles and not the anus. You can also try the reverse, contracting only the anus while focusing on not contracting the PC muscles as well. This isolation technique takes practice, but it is a great way to increase your awareness and strengthen these muscles both physically and energetically, helping to overall strengthen the energy in the lower chakra areas.

Grounding: The Crucial Foundation

I have to offer a huge caveat: all the pleasure power center work in the world will not work for you unless you know how to ground yourself.

My extreme dizziness involved two factors. First, I still had too much energy in my head. Second, I was nine months into a dive deep into feminine/masculine energy work, but nobody had taught me about the importance of grounding all the powerful energy that I was learning to unlock and unleash. When you start activating and circulating powerful life-force energy throughout your body, it can overwhelm your physical and energetic system if you don't know how to ground yourself and your energy.

Grounding is not optional if you are serious about this work. It's absolutely necessary.

One of my favorite parts of yoga is being barefoot and in direct connection with the floor. Savasana, the pose in which you lie on the floor with your entire body making contact with the surface beneath you, is even better. If your feet touching the ground produces amazing results, sitting or lying on the floor is even more beneficial. There is something incredibly comforting about being able to completely let go and let the earth hold you.

You can achieve great clarity by simply connecting with the earth. This is why it works wonders for so many people to go out in nature, go for a walk, a run, a hike, or a swim, or visit the mountains or forest. Removing yourself from man-made materials and contraptions, which can act as interference between you and the Universe, brings deep serenity. When you can be in direct connection with the planet, you are more likely to feel, peace, clarity, and inspiration.

There's a practice called "earthing" that simply entails going outside and finding some grass, sand, or dirt so that you can remove your shoes and connect with the ground, using your bare feet, with the intention of truly connecting with a source of healing power. During any grounding practice, focus on bringing energy up through your feet and legs and into your body, spreading the loving, healing light energy of mother earth.

When my dizziness was at its worst, I can remember instinctively wanting to go outside barefoot and just stand in one place on the dirt where I felt comfortable and stable. This was before I ever heard of earthing. Other times, I felt drawn to sit on my bedroom or living-room floor. Sometimes sitting wasn't enough: I had to lie down on the floor. When even that wasn't enough to calm the spinning, I would put some of my heavy crystals on top of my body to weigh me down even more.

In my darkest moments during the bout with the dizziness, I sought refuge in a particular spot in my front yard, facing the Sandia Mountain Range, northeast of Albuquerque, NM.

Not only would I stand there barefoot, I would really dig my feet into the soil and concentrate on bringing in feelings of groundedness.

Feeling your feet on the floor is a big component. The way your feet hit the ground is so important: that connection is key. Pay attention to how your feet connect with the floor and the earth, not just during a meditation or mindfulness practice but as you walk around doing your everyday activities.

Grounding Techniques:

- **Earthing** is the practice of connecting with the earth with your bare feet. Walking barefoot on dirt, grass, rock, or sand, for example, is a great way to naturally and effortlessly help clear nervous energy that is swirling around in your head or in your body.

  Any time your bare feet or skin come in contact with the ground, free electrons are conducted and circulated throughout your body. These free electrons are nature's antioxidants and help neutralize free radicals that can harm the body and lead to various ailments and disease.

- **Toe Tapping** is a simple exercise that you can do almost anywhere and requires no equipment but has huge benefits for the entire body, energetic system, and your natural grounding ability.

  - Simply lie on the floor with your arms at your sides and with your legs and heels of your feet touching. Then tap the bones below each big toe together repeatedly. If it is comfortable for you to do so, feel free to tap them together with a good amount of force, creating a tapping sound each time they meet. Continue this practice for at least two minutes, ideally at least twice per day.

- When you have completed your tapping repetitions, lie still for as long as you need to relax into your body as you visualize any negative, stagnant energy exiting your body through your fingers and toes. Breathe naturally and deeply.

- Toe tapping helps to cool your head, clear your energy, balance your energy meridians, and cleanse your physical and energetic body of any negative stagnant energy, relieving stress and calming the mind and nervous system.

- **Rock Grounding** is an exercise used by elite professional athletes, who know how important it is to feel solidly connected to the ground in order to move, react, and respond effectively and efficiently.

  - The practice is simple. All you need is a smooth rock. Find yourself a smooth rock about the size of a clam shell. Place it underneath your foot, and press your foot down onto it, creating pressure against your sole.

  - Adjust the placement of your foot, trying to find the most sensitive, tender spot you can find. Once you do, press your weight down on the rock even harder. Continue to put pressure on your foot against the rock for at least one minute. Then, slowly remove your foot from the rock and gently place it back on the floor. Feel the difference. Note how this foot and this side of your body feel different from the other side.

  - Switch feet and repeat the above steps on your other foot.

  - Place both feet firmly on the ground and take a few moments to ground both feet into the ground even further.

Walk around for a few moments, noticing what feels different and how this exercise affects the rest of your body. Many important meridians (or energy lines) run through the feet; this practice can activate those meridians and improve the function of your body and nervous system. By focusing on the feeling in your feet, you can also draw down any busy, distracting, head bubble energy.

When you feel like you have a solid foundation on which to stand, you give the rest of your body permission to come out and play. Your physical and energetic body is like a house: in order for it to stand tall and function well, it must have a rock-solid foundation. If you do this exercise before going out and interacting with people, you will likely feel more present, more aware, and more expressive with the rest of your body. Your body is the vehicle for your soul and it can help you be fully expressed when it is grounded, and your mind is out of your head bubble. When there is safety and stability in your foundation, you will experience more confidence, more stability, less mental fog and clutter and you will feel more freedom to move and express yourself.

- **Focus on Gravity.** Simply paying attention to and appreciating gravity can help you normalize your energetic condition, bring busy energy down from your head, and help contain the life-force energy you create using the power center strengthening exercises in this chapter. You've probably had moments where you've stood up too fast from bending over or lying down and have experienced the sensation of a brief period of dizziness that requires you to remain still while the energy in your body normalizes so you can regain your balance. During that time, energy is coming down from your head and redistributing back down into your body.

Recall this feeling. Imagine that you have just stood up from bending over and focus your attention on what happens when your energy starts to settle. Even though you haven't really bent over and stood up, you will still find that with your focus and awareness, you are able to allow energy to settle down into your body. Notice energy leaving your busy head space and allow it to collect into your power center and down into your legs to your feet and into the ground.

Focus your attention on gravity and how it helps bring your energy down any time, not just when you stand or sit up too quickly to balance and ground your energy.

Being grounded gives your body and your spirit the stability and safety.

Without that, nothing else matters; you have nothing to build on.

With that, your body and soul's playing field becomes vast and electrifying.

HEART:

*Activate Your Heart Center
for Maximum Magnetism*

CHAPTER 7

Clear the Channel

For maximum benefit, the life-force energy you cultivate in your pleasure power center must be able to circulate throughout your body and energetic system. It can't travel to your upper chakras if you have blockages in your heart area. Clearing and cleansing your heart energy center will also allow you to radiate compassionate, vulnerable, loving energy that will complement the power and intensity of your pleasure power center.

Our built-in protection mechanisms cause us to instinctively protect our heart: it's part survival instinct and part conditioning from past hurt to protect ourselves from heartbreak, pain, and embarrassment. We tend to build up an energetic armor, sometimes to protect ourselves and sometimes because we think we need it to project a strong confident persona. But one of the key ingredients to developing mind-blowing magnetism is the willingness to be human and share the parts of ourselves that most people are unwilling to bare to the world. To do this, we must chip away at this armor so that people can experience the version of you that lives beneath the protective layer that you've built up.

Compassion is Crucial

I've met several women who were very tapped into their feminine energy and exuded sex appeal, sensuality, and power, but who also could be described as intimidating. The same is true for men: I've met confident men who exude a powerful, assertive, energy, but who lack the kind of warmth and approachability that makes people feel comfortable and safe around them.

Men and women who are unable to balance their powerful energy and confidence with warmth often have some sort of heart space blockages and haven't done the work to heal and open their hearts. This energy can read as intimidation and unapproachability.

Arriving at the energetic sweet spot means that you can simultaneously radiate power and confidence with love and compassion. Tremendous power must be tempered with tremendous compassion, love, and understanding.

When you tap into your divine source of primal energy while also opening your heart chakra, this allows the energy to travel smoothly from one energy center to the next.

Embrace the Discomfort

In order to help the heat and energy in our power center communicate with our heart center, we must clear the channel. What's clogging it?

- Energetic blockages in the body

- Emotions that are stuck in our bodies

- "Negative" thoughts and emotions that we aren't willing to allow, invite, or face

- Unresolved inner conflicts

- Unhealed past traumas

When we make progress in the areas above, we create a clearer channel. Our bodies and energetic systems become unhindered and unpolluted so that we can feel more deeply. We can experience pleasure, joy, happiness, and aliveness on a deeper level. In order to feel these pleasurable emotions, we must be willing to feel the rest of our feelings and emotions, even the uncomfortable and unpleasant ones.

If we don't, we become detached from our physical bodies and emotional bodies because we are trying to escape from our real lives into an imaginary world where everything is okay. The fantasy of a quick fix is tempting: we want relief and we want it now. We want to focus on the symptoms of the discomfort instead of the underlying causes. We live in a culture where that is a reasonable expectation to most.

Phenomenal advances in modern medicine save lives every day; I am grateful for doctors, surgeons, healers, and specialists who are committed to improving our health. But in many instances, drugs, treatments, and medicines are dispensed that address symptoms instead of the underlying causes. And many illnesses have emotional or traumatic underlying causes that medicine alone will never resolve.

Many people love a quick fix or a magic bullet; few are interested in how we can heal ourselves. It can take longer, and sometimes it requires more time, energy, financial resources, and effort, and we have to be willing to sit with the discomfort a little longer. But that is the beauty of healing ourselves naturally. When we heal ourselves, we have more long-lasting results because we are not simply putting a bandage over the issue. When you are willing to do deep healing and self-discovery work, life-changing transformation takes place.

How do we experience difficult emotions without letting them take over? We must trust that the experience will take us farther down the road that leads to more enjoyment, joy, and pleasure. If we do not go through them, the challenging emotions will always be there, taking up space and energy because they've never been properly experienced. They've only been pushed down, patched over, and have been ignored and uninvited, which makes these emotions hungrier for attention. They are trying to tell you something, to send you insight that will help you rise above and make it to the next place in your personal and spiritual growth. They are trying to lead you to a place where you will be best prepared to deal with what comes next.

When we are able to fully experience these emotions, we see how it was all necessary, part of the divine process. When you process an emotion or traumatic event, it will likely feel satisfying or freeing in some way. And while we might feel like we're done clearing our emotions, even though we may achieve and enjoy states of clarity, balance, and perspective along the way, our job of clearing our energy and emotions is never really finished. We must continue to peel back the layers, but we will never finish interfacing with our "bad" emotions because this is part of a fully awakened, fully functional life. A diversity of emotional experience colors our lives. We need contrast.

We need a range of emotions. We can use them as a compass, letting them lead the way. These pain points draw a map of the bumps along the way, the landmarks, the milestones, the learning points. We don't need to step over them. We don't need to walk around them or make sure that we never encounter them. In fact, we need to do the opposite: we need to welcome them and encounter them with full faith that they are of value and that we can learn much about what within us needs to be healed.

We become more efficient as we dive into these landmark places again and again. As we practice, we are less prone to getting consumed by our emotions. We are less likely to get trapped in a downward spiral into self-loathing, judgment, despair, and hopelessness. We enter each shadowed moment with more clarity than the last, with a kind of confidence that this isn't our "forever" place; this is just the place where we can take a good, hard look in the mirror and acknowledge the parts of ourselves that seek acceptance, love, and the benefit of a new perspective. We enter, knowing that once we deal with this directly, we will leave this place with newfound strength, experience, and wisdom that will serve us in ways we never imagined.

First, we cultivate the willingness to go there. The bravery and the courage to say, *I am not afraid of the dark. There is much to be learned there. This is my continuum and all the colors along this continuum are for me and I want this. Teach me about life. Teach me about myself. Show me my strength. Show me the rhyme and reason so that I can go out and teach others not to be afraid of the dark. So that I can go out and teach others that every part of them, every experience, every emotion and supposed shortcoming is a beautiful part of their collage.* Every experience is made of many brilliant parts and each one shines in a different way, there to teach a different lesson and reveal a different part of life and a different facet of who you are.

Feel Your Dahn-jon Deeper

For at least a year and a half, every night I would listen to the same meditation designed to be heard right before I fall asleep. It worked like a charm. It relaxed me and helped me release the events of the day and clear my energy so that I could have a restful night. Before I discovered the meditation, I could sleep through the night once I'd finally fallen asleep, but when I first lay down, mind chatter bombarded me. All of a sudden, everything that happened throughout the day would tumble into my mind, especially if I hadn't had the chance to deal with it or process it yet. Sometimes, I would get up and journal; that would often help me clear my head. But at other times, sheer exhaustion or an impending early wake-up in the morning kept me from journaling — I just wanted to fall asleep. The meditation recording offered a way to stop the mental chatter by giving me something else to focus on that was calming, eventually lulling me to sleep. It helped me turn off the thousands of thoughts in my brain, but it didn't make them go away forever. So, while this meditation was great for unwinding and falling asleep, the same worries and concerns were there the next day.

But then one day, I stopped. I didn't need it anymore. I had a new practice I could use anytime I felt distracted or restless. This new practice didn't require an audio track or headphones: it relied on nothing and nobody except me.

I made the change overnight while staying at a cute little bed and breakfast in Topanga, California. I was in town for a photo shoot for a collaborative book to which I was contributing. About 15 of the other contributors were staying together in a large house; I'd opted for my own lodging, because as an extreme introvert, staying in a house with 10 other women, no matter how amazing and wonderful, sounded energetically draining, and I wanted to be prepared for the intimate photo shoot.

Our assignment was to choose poses and wardrobe that highlighted our femininity, vulnerability, freedom, and power, therefore many women wore minimal clothing, and some opted for nudity. I was excited for an opportunity to play dress-up. I had always thought it would be fun to dress up like a warrior princess with a real sword, and this was my chance! I was also nervous — I would be wearing only a loin cloth and a piece of fur over my shoulders, barely covering my breasts. I had never been photographed wearing so little before. I wasn't in bikini model shape, but I was committed to being an example of a powerful woman who is able to let go of insecurities and perfectionist tendencies in favor of self-expression and unconditional self-love.

But the photo shoot was not as much fun as I'd imagined. We were on a strict time schedule, and I was second-to-last on a full day of sessions. The photographer — one I'd never worked with before — seemed frustrated with me. She wasn't happy with the vulnerable, strong, feminine poses I was trying.

She said, "I need more from you. Be raw." What did that mean? Her words discouraged me. She called me over to look at the preview screen of her camera. She said, "Look. Does this look good to you?" I had to admit that no, it did not look good. I was looking at an extremely unflattering photo of myself.

It was challenging to walk back in front of the lights and the camera and re-center myself and remind myself that I was beautiful and amazing and that I could continue for the duration of the one-hour session.

It was one of the longest hours of my life, uncomfortable and confronting.

I was relieved when it was over and was instantly uplifted when I connected behind the scenes with my dear friend who was also being photographed that day. We hugged and laughed, we took selfies, and then she took some pictures of me with my phone. Her loving and playful spirit made me smile and produced some really great photos that captured my personality. Looking at those amateur photos makes me realize there was nothing wrong with me during the official photo shoot; I just needed to work with someone who could relate with me and who was a strong vibrational match.

I felt frustrated with how the photo shoot had gone. I had been envisioning a fun, empowering experience. It definitely wasn't fun for me, but looking back on it now, I realize that it was still empowering — just not in the way I'd expected. The old me would have started crying or stormed off in frustration to demonstrate my discontent. Instead, thanks to the techniques in this book, I stayed grounded in my pleasure power center, which helped me stay present and calm and do the absolute best I could do, given the circumstances.

Back in my room that night, I was glad the day was over. Just as my body began to relax, I realized that I had to return the next day for the group photo. I'd have to go back and work with the same photographer with a smile on my face.

I woke up feeling better but not fully renewed. I was still feeling the draining energetic and emotional effects of the experience the day before. My eyes were red. I looked tired and I was still dealing with the stress-related pimples that had popped up leading to the photo shoot. After waiting as long as possible, I arrived at the photo-shoot location and discovered they were running an hour and a half behind. Still drained, I could not believe that I was stuck in the house without a way to recharge, refresh, and re-ignite.

To my delight, that same friend whom I played with behind the photo set suggested that we both take a nap to pass the time. A chance to close my eyes and meditate sounded perfect. The only remaining option in the house was a twin bed for us to share in a pass-through room in the middle of the house.

Okay, I can still work with this, I thought. At least I could lie still with my eyes closed and not talk to anyone. As we lay down, my friend nuzzled up to me and said, "I hope you don't mind, but I'm a snuggler." I had to smile at the cascading challenges; could I re-ground, re-center, and connect to my true and resilient spirit under such circumstances?

I closed my eyes and brought my attention to my pleasure power center. After a year and a half of practice, I knew I could do this, but I surprised myself with how well. In a recent healing meditation session with Master Hongik, she asked me to speak out loud any thoughts, worries, and concerns as we tapped our dahn-jons. After each thought, worry, or concern, she had us repeat the phrase, "But, I choose to feel my dahn-jon deeper."

Lying in bed amidst the chaos and sensory input of my friend's snuggles, I connected to that magical place within myself without tapping, and recited in my head, "I'm feeling insecure about my ability to *shine shine shine* in front of the camera. But, I choose to feel my dahn-jon deeper." "I'm tired and I don't feel like getting up and smiling. But, I choose to feel my dahn-jon deeper." "I can't focus with all this noise in this house. But, I choose to feel my dahn-jon deeper." As I said the words, I imagined that I was literally inserting my fears, doubts, and insecurities into my pleasure power center, a place of great power, heat, and energy that can handle anything. Magical and divine, my power center transformed, dissolved, and dissipated my fears and worries.

I rose from my side of that twin bed as cleansed and refreshed as if I'd slept for 12 peaceful hours, even though it had only been about 30 minutes.

After that day, I never relied on my guided sleep meditation again. Instead, I can now intentionally experience my entire range of emotions more quickly and deeply by shedding my armor, opening myself up, and letting my pleasure power center transmute difficult emotions or experiences.

> ## EXERCISE: TRANSFORM WORRY TO WISDOM
>
> *Think of a current worry, fear, concern, question, or challenge.*
>
> *Close your eyes.*
>
> *Project the thing that you thought of onto an imaginary movie screen in front of you.*
>
> *Then, bring your challenge, fear, worry, question, or concern into your head, behind your eyes. Welcome it in and imagine that it is descending into your body through an imaginary tube, making its way down to rest in your pleasure power center. As if you are swallowing it.*

> *Use your breath and your focus to engage your power center (using your sphere of light, or whatever imagery calls to you) to intensify your relationship and connection to this space within your body.*
>
> *Feel the sensations that swirl in your pelvic region as it handles what you have entrusted it to handle for you. Feel the heat. Feel the non-resistance. Feel your emotions and thoughts begin to transform. Continue to breathe deeply, sending air and energy down your body straight into your pleasure power center.*
>
> *Pause, and take a physical, mental and energetic inventory. Note any changes in your nervousness and stress or worry levels.*
>
> *Gently open your eyes when you're ready. Notice how you feel after using the strength of your pleasure power center to handle those things that at first can seem daunting and unmanageable.*

Clear Energetic Blockages in the Body

When you speak, you're not just talking with your words; you're using your entire body. You're like a performer telling a story; people pick up your body language and energy even if they don't realize it.

You have to be a clear energy channel or else there's a disconnect — and people have built-in bullshit detectors. This doesn't mean you're intentionally dishing out bullshit — trying to manipulate or trick anyone — it just means there are some unconscious pieces below the surface, which are out of alignment with your conscious mind's communication. That dissonance can be picked up. And if they don't trust your body language, they won't trust you. Even if I think I'm hiding something from my past, it is living in my body.

"It's a Good Thing You Have a Mouth"

I lay face down on a massage table, and a man called the "Soul Whisperer" pressed and dug into my body in places I had no idea could feel so much tenderness and sensation. He pressed with intention, knowing there was something in my body that needed to emerge into the light — even if it hurt at first. As uncomfortable as it was, I was thrilled to be there. I had been waiting for this session and I knew that it was going to be a powerful experience for me.

I was sobbing and crying during our session; so hard that my nose became so stopped up that I had to breathe through my mouth. He kept working on the tender spot in my mid-to-upper left back and shoulder area. I told him, "I can't breathe through my nose." He gave me a Kleenex and said, "Well then, it's a good thing you have a mouth," and continued his work.

The pain was laced with pleasure because my wise soul knew I was diving in to do some deep healing. My upper back and shoulders were so tender because I'd been carrying so much grief and guilt from years ago. Before he'd begun working on these areas, I had told the Soul Whisperer a story that still haunted me.

When my daughter was about nine months old, my husband and I took her on a family vacation. At the late-night conclusion of our return flight, we fumbled with all our luggage at our home airport. My daughter sat in the stroller while my husband and I struggled with all the bags and equipment needed to travel with a baby: stroller, car seat, diaper bag, luggage, etc. Without thinking about how flexible the top cover of the stroller was, I tried to rest the base of the car seat against the top handle of the stroller. I accidentally struck the back of her head with the car seat base, a ridiculously heavy piece of metal and plastic. She cried and cried in my arms for a long time. We went directly to the emergency room from the airport, a ride that felt hours long but probably took 15 minutes. Worry and concern choked me. Had I permanently injured her?

They examined her and sent us home, saying she was fine but to keep an eye on her for the next 12 hours to watch for anything concerning. I couldn't believe I had been so careless. I felt like the worst mother and a stupid human being.

Eleven years later, I cried as I told the Soul Whisperer this story. He reflected back to me what was happening: I had spent more than a decade beating myself up for an accident, forcing myself to carry the guilt for not being a better, more careful mom. I was using that story as a weapon against myself, turning it into a symbol of me as a bad, inattentive mother; telling the story that I am stupid, irresponsible, and without common sense.

On one level, it sounds crazy, to spend 11 years degrading myself because of an accident that had no lingering ill effects. On another level, I know how common this is — to beat ourselves up about things long past, even though we know there is no benefit to doing so. An unconscious and unempowering pattern of thought takes hold that you want to stop but can't.

Sometimes it feels like the more you tell yourself to stop, the more momentum you give the negative thought cycle. Once you cease resisting, the space clears for you to simply notice the negative thoughts, send them on their way, thanking them for sharing, and refocus on incorporating the truth of who you are into every cell of your body.

Embodiment is about becoming so in tune with your body that you can recognize when you're carrying emotions in your physical body. The more you can do this, the better you will be positioned to get quiet, connect with yourself, connect with the loving energy of the Universe, and wrap yourself in the unconditional love and support that can bring you back from feeling inadequate.

After my session with the Soul Whisperer, I left feeling as if a tremendous weight had been lifted off me. My chest was open, my shoulders were settled back, and I walked and breathed with a new kind of lightness. Who knew that crying so much could eventually make you feel so good?

Over the last couple of years, I've become fascinated by how important the events in our lives are and how they shape how we think, feel, and act. If you are curious and would like to learn more, I recommend the work of Dr. Deborah Sandella, including her RIM (Regenerating Images through Memory) technique and her book *Goodbye, Hurt and Pain: 7 Simple Steps for Health, Love and Success*, or *The Body Keeps the Score: Brain, Mind and Body in the Healing of Trauma* by Bessel van der Kolk M.D.

Your body is always communicating with you. Are you listening?

Don't be afraid of what you'll uncover. Your instincts will guide you to the work you are ready to do for yourself. If there are deep wounds and trauma, they will only surface when it's time and in your highest and best interest to do so.

If you are willing to work with and deal with your own guilt, shame, insecurities, and emotional wounds and blocks, you will create the space within that allows you to see yourself clearly so you can serve as your own source of love, compassion, and inspiration.

When your vessel is cloudy, it's difficult to see your own brilliance.

When it's clear, when you invest time in continually checking to see what needs to be cleared out, you can see your own brilliance and potential. You can also see it in others with a kind of clarity that will allow you to reflect back what you see. When it comes from a place that has been purified in this manner of mental and emotional clearing, it will be received as genuine feedback that says, "This is simply what is and I am reflecting that back to you." When people hear things shared in this tone, they are able to receive it fully.

EXERCISE: RELEASE SHAME AND GUILT

If you could take an X-ray of the experiences, traumatic events, regrets, resentments, emotions, and memories stored in your body, what would you see?

Is there something within you that you have convinced yourself you have forgotten that still lingers somewhere, layers below the surface?

As you consider these memories, ask yourself:

What do you think you cannot say?

What do you think is un-utterable?

Whatever your answer, say it, speak it — whether in your car alone, on a piece of paper that you then burn, or out loud to a safe loved one.

Clear your heart center and enjoy the euphoria of shedding that which you thought was stuck forever. Know that in doing so, not only do you heal yourself, you inspire and enable others to heal themselves by releasing old stories about themselves.

Only You Can Fill the Hole

I sat in an audience of women at a personal-development workshop when a woman stood up and said she was thinking of leaving her husband. She felt like something was missing; a dark sadness lingered in her heart, and her husband had recently said to her, "There is a hole in your heart and I don't think I will ever be able to fill it for you."

Silence and stillness settled on the room after she spoke. It felt like most of us had felt like this at some point in our lives, including me. I was struggling in my own marriage and feeling confused. I waited anxiously for the facilitator to speak.

Would she advise her to leave her husband? Seek marriage counseling? Visualize meeting her soul mate? She didn't say any of those things. Instead, she told the woman — she told all of us — that if you have a hole in your heart, there isn't anyone out there who can fill it. Nobody can complete you. You have to complete yourself. The room was perfectly silent for a few moments.

I don't know how that woman's story ended but hearing part of her story made me realize that I had been blaming my husband for not making me feel how I wanted to feel. I blamed him for not filling the part of me that felt somehow dark, empty, and incomplete. Romantic fairytales have a way of making us believe there is someone out there who can fill that void. Yes, there are people who can help you on your journey. But there is no one person who holds the answer to making you feel healed and complete. It's an inside job that you can't outsource to anyone. If your reason to be happy is a person, you are at the mercy of your connection with them.

I have learned that the most powerful and fulfilling relationships are comprised of two people who feel perfect, whole, and complete all by themselves; who then come together to experience each other and share their energy without dependence.

There are so many people out there who are searching for someone to make them whole and who think that finding the perfect person for them will solve everything.

Fall in love with yourself first. Commit to diving deep into personal development. Embrace your longing, sadness, and imperfection. Welcome it. It's there for a reason: as you face and overcome those sore places, you will become increasingly aware, full of self-esteem, and able to love with a warm heart while beaming with pride about your perfectly imperfect self.

Without self-love, you will never realize the deepest capacity to love another. Without self-love, you will never fully realize your dreams, goals, and visions. Self-love is foundational. There is no person, achievement, or relationship that will fill that hole, except for you.

As we explored in Part One, you can learn to identify and reproduce the positive, uplifting, turned-on feelings that certain people evoke. You can practice cultivating that energy yourself. This doesn't mean that you don't need anybody, or that real love and connection and soul mates and all of that good stuff doesn't exist. It means that you will feel happier and much more powerful and able to manifest things in your life when you experience your own capacity to generate from within that kind of unconditional love, support, and admiration. You can do it by meditating and become adept in your practice of bringing in life, god, mother earth, divine energy and using it to heal yourself, using it to pour love all over yourself and realizing that it lives in you, that you are a part of something bigger and have access to infinite love, wisdom, strength, stamina, endurance, and clarity.

Techniques for Shedding Your Armor

Unlocking tension and blockages in the heart can help us release grief, anger, and resentment because this is the area where theses emotions tend to get stuck in the body. Opening the energy channels and chakras in the body allow the energy to flow freely from one area or energy center of the body to the others. Many of us have blockages in certain key areas of the body, like the heart/chest area, neck and shoulders, and second and third chakras, which correspond to your source of willpower and your primal sexual energy.

Blockages can occur anywhere, though. Physical movement helps to unstick some of the blockages, but we have to move in ways that we don't typically move. Dancing is great for this, ideally something free-flowing like ecstatic dance; it helps you become comfortable moving your body in non-habitual ways. You can go to a class, and you can also have a dance party on your own — as long as you stick with it even if you feel silly. Put together a kickass playlist of songs that make you want to move, then just start moving and let the music take you … wherever it wants to take you.

When we move and stimulate our chests, energy flows back to the heart chakra area, and you get another happy byproduct: firmer breasts or pectoral muscles as a result of the extra stimulation and increase in blood circulation. I use a tapping technique similar to the one discussed in the Pleasure Power Center chapter.

CHEST OPENING EXERCISES

Chest Area Tapping

Using your fingertips, tap on and around your chest area to wake up the energy there. Be sure to include your underarms, collarbone, ribcage, and shoulders to open up the entire space around your chest. Use varying levels of pressure depending on what feels good. Tap on and around your chest area for at least two minutes to promote healing and circulation. Note: Women will experience the best results by performing this exercise without a bra on.

Chest Massage

You can perform a chest or breast massage on yourself, or teach your partner(s) to do it.

First, get into a relaxed physical position and state of mind — maybe turn on some meditation music, mantra music, or a sensual playlist. Consider using coconut oil to enhance your hands' ability to glide smoothly on and around your chest in gentle, delicate, circling motions for as long as you desire.

When you get ready to do some breast massage, keep the pressure light and gentle, as the nipples are very sensitive. Start with caressing and circular movements around the breasts, slowly making your way to the outer edges, working your way in, drawing it out, until finally you can begin to touch your nipples. Begin softly and slowly, you can progress to putting more pressure or pinching them for maximum stimulation. While you're performing your breast aliveness exercise, see if you can be in conscious appreciation for what it feels like to be "in your body" and to not have your awareness dominated primarily by mental activity.

These chest-opening exercises will allow the powerful life-force energy generated in your pleasure power center to heal and radiate out from your heart, your head, and the rest of your body. It will also give you an increased capacity to feel love and experience compassion and gratitude.

Chest Breathing

Lie flat on the floor with your arms out to your sides. Extend them out at about a 45-degree angle and allow your legs and feet to be completely relaxed. Begin to focus on the sound of your own breath.

Bring to your attention and awareness the rise and fall of your chest as you inhale and exhale.

Imagine that above you there is a beautiful, pure source of water flowing down and entering your body through the center of your chest.

Invite this cleansing water energy to work its way through the muscles, fibers, bones, and crevices in your body. Envision that this water energy flows into your chest and then out through your arms and fingertips, cleansing your energy, muscles, and emotions as it flows. Once you get in the rhythm of this practice and begin to relax into it, slow things down and on your exhalations, visualize the water and the stagnant energy that it is ushering out of your body leaving through one finger at a time. You can begin with either hand, taking ten full rounds of complete breaths to release, soften, and clear your energy.

> ### *Heart Opening Meditation*
>
> *Relax your shoulders, slow your breathing, and focus on the movement of your ribs as you breathe in and out. Focus not only on the front of your body but also extend your focus, attention, and feeling to the back of your chest as well. Many people have constructed an invisible armor to protect their hearts. Imagine for a moment what your armor looks and feels like. How thick or thin is it? What is it made of? What color is it? Are there any designs on it? Now imagine that you are able to easily and swiftly take off your chest armor so that you can feel movement and freedom in your chest and the back of your chest.*
>
> *Invite love to enter your heart. Invite forgiveness. Visualize green energy encircling your sacred heart space and protecting you in a loving, open way that shields you from negative energy without preventing compassion and positive energy from flowing in and out.*

Jealousy is a Call to Action

Jealousy is typically thought to be an "undesirable" feeling. Common advice is to shift your focus to gratitude and focus on what you DO have. So many people have been trained to try to stop feeling emotions like jealousy, resentment, frustration, and dissatisfaction.

I like to take the opposite approach. I love the process of leaning in to these kinds of "bad" feelings. If we sugarcoat our feelings, we end up missing out on what they're trying to tell us and where they're trying to lead us. If I chastise myself, "Oh, Michelle, you shouldn't feel jealous," I'm rejecting part of myself that's crying out and trying to say something, probably something worthwhile.

As a personal example, I once noticed that jealousy and feelings of "not being good enough" crept into my heart when

I read social media posts from an acquaintance who was experiencing great success as a coach, speaker, and author — all of which are things I love to do and always want to get better at. I wondered, "Do I not have enough motivation, talent, or perseverance?" "Am I not meant for that kind of success?"

The more I paid attention to the emotions arising inside, the more I realized that the reason her success struck such a deep chord within is that I also want my material, my posts, my articles to be visible, to be heard. Then I saw the words "Jealousy Is A Call To Action," and immediately understood: my envy was a compass needle pointing to my deepest desires and capacity.

I started to use jealousy as a sign. That's how we're built, this is how the Universe and our souls speak to us: when we have some dormant possibility and capability inside, we will experience strong triggers.

As soon as I shifted my focus from jealousy to my own aspirations and desires, I was filled with possibility and determination. I no longer wanted to be "better than her." I just wanted to know I was expressing myself and accomplishing things to the best of my ability, making use of all my latent ideas, energy, and momentum that I had and was capable of generating.

Jealousy is okay. Jealousy is more than okay. Jealousy can light a fire in some way; it can move you into action, it can guide you and give you clues about what you want and about what you don't want. Commit to digging deep and learning what about this person or this situation triggers your envy. What does it remind you that you don't have? What if you really embraced your jealousy and found a way to enjoy the feelings it produces by focusing on what it shows you about what you desire?

Jealousy has intensity — learn to use the power behind it. Jealousy is natural. You can't control it. But you CAN control what you do after you notice yourself experiencing it.

Many of us just want to make it go away and to tell our-selves things like, "Focus on yourself," "Stay in your own lane," "It's not spiritually evolved to be jealous." But even if your mind agrees with those statements, you're still left with the feeling. The most powerful thing you can do is to transmute the powerful energy behind it. It's much easier to redirect it than it is to try to make it disappear.

Jealous of something someone has? Focus on WHY you want that and what it is that you think having it will bring you. What will you experience as a result of getting it? Focus on the feeling you'd get versus the fact that you don't have it. Resist jumping to problem-solving, figuring out HOW you're going to get there. Resist focusing on the tangible result and ask yourself, "How will getting _________ make me feel?" This opens up your perspective; there are multiple ways to achieve that feeling, which is really what your subconscious self longs for.

You don't even have to get "the thing" as long as you can practice channeling these kinds of feelings and learning how to hold on to them like muscle memory. This skill is called "holding the charge of desire," something that we practice in The Art of Feminine Presence, but which is relevant for everyone. Staying in this state of being will help attract the things and circumstances you want (which may be different from what you thought you wanted, by the way.)

Dark Shadow Identification

In an inverse manner, the traits, characteristics and hab-its that bother you most about other people are usually the same things that you are denying about yourself. They are parts of you that you have disowned or try to push away. We suppress certain parts of ourselves because at some moment in our lives, we got the message that these parts were bad or unacceptable. But when we ignore or push away parts of us, they don't disappear and after being repressed for so long, they will usually show up with intensity at times when we are highly triggered or have an intense emotional response. It's like an emotional volcano erupting.

One of the best ways to identify the shadow parts of yourself is to pay attention to what triggers, upsets, or offends you about other people. Typically, this gives you a good idea of what attitudes or behaviors you feel are unacceptable and thus have not allowed yourself to embrace or demonstrate. One of the ways to work with this is to identify how the trait, characteristic, or habit that irritates can sometimes be beneficial. How can you view the quality as something valuable, even if only at certain times or in particular circumstances?

Incorporating our shadow is an important part of cultivating self-love because it helps us love, embrace, and accept all parts of ourselves. Shadow traits or behaviors also contain aspects that, when embraced, can serve a good purpose. For example, if someone gets enraged when a friend behaves in a selfish manner, it may be either that they've never allowed themselves to exhibit selfishness or that they often behave selfishly but aren't aware of it. If this person works with the shadow of selfishness, it may come to light that they give so fully that they have prioritized other people's needs over their own, to devastating results on their health. For someone like this, it would benefit their emotional and physical well-being to make a conscious attempt to be more selfish, even though many people would label this as a "bad" characteristic. A selfish-acting person attends to their needs, and when they are well taken care of, they will be in a better position to serve others.

EXERCISE: IDENTIFY ONE OF YOUR SHADOWS

We can look for shadow traits in a few different ways. First, ask yourself what people do that tends to push your buttons. Or, ask yourself: What is the one characteristic you would be horrified if someone declared to be true about you, then screamed it from the rooftops? What is that thing? It is probably a characteristic or attribute. Are you that? If we have a strong emotional response to this it can mean one of two things – first, it can mean that deep down you really believe this about yourself. Or that you are so determined not to be this thing that you are in denial that this could be true about you some of the time. And both can be true as well. So, in either case, you have some personal work to do.

Alternately, you can make a list of three to five of your positive qualities that you're proud of. Then, beside each positive quality, identify its opposite. For example, if you listed "being independent," beside that quality you would list "being dependent," or if you listed "generous," you would write "greedy" beside it.

Sit in meditation and focus on allowing your shadow to be present. Have a conversation with your shadow. Ask what it wants. Tell it that it is okay to show itself. Ask what it is trying to teach you.

Think of a particular shadow you've identified, then answer the following questions about it.

- *Can you identify an instance when you demonstrated this quality?*
- *Where were you?*
- *Who were you with?*
- *What happened?*
- *Can you think of some ways in which demonstrating this quality might actually be a good thing?*

It Hurts So Good

It's uniquely satisfying to face your fears, reveal hidden truths, speak aloud what you've been ashamed of, and open yourself up in new ways.

Personal development work includes so many "feel good" moments, but it is by no means all sunshine and rainbows. We dig deep, we get super vulnerable, brutally honest, and soul-expanding expressive. We learn to fall in love with even the painful processes of confronting self-discovery. Things are being uncovered and unleashed and that is what happens when you start to unlock the unconscious.

Magic is about fusing together the conscious and the subconscious.

Carolyn Elliott, writer and business maven, teaches a process called "existential kink." Very briefly, she explains, "The end of suffering is the willingness to enjoy overwhelming sensation (i.e. pain) rather than trying to push it away." Existential kink has its theoretical roots in traditional BDSM (bondage, discipline, sadism and masochism) where participants take pleasure from experiencing pain. When we can take pleasure in the struggle and pain of personal and professional development, we experience the process as a colorful, multidimensional experience. And this pleasure prepares us for all the twists and turns in real life instead of simply trying to "stay positive" all the time.

It's uniquely pleasurable to be in a state of being where you have range and freedom to experience exhilaration, wonderment, vitality, somberness, sensitivity, anger, joy, anticipation, darkness, elation, and all other emotions on the spectrum. It feels good to fully experience ranges of emotion without censoring or putting a positive spin on them.

Be willing to get messy; go deep. Welcome it all in and wake up and shake things up so you can feel more alive and aware than ever, using these amplified powers to show up as multi-dimensional creatures who are thoroughly enjoying every unpredictable step.

CHAPTER 8

Letting Go of Self-Consciousness

Who Are You When You Think Nobody Is Watching?

About 10 years ago, when my daughter Talia was five years old, her grandparents had taken her for the weekend, which gave me and my husband Brian a chance to sleep in. I woke up around 9:30 a.m., drove to Starbucks in my pajamas, and took my half-caff americano back home to start our lazy TV marathon. One of those cheesy Lifetime movies was on, where the man is leading a double-life and his wife finds out and you know what's going to happen next but you can't stop watching. During commercial breaks, I did a few loads of laundry. As I was walking down the hallway, laundry basket on my hip, Brian called out from the office, "Hey, psst, Michelle, come here. Look what I did. Look."

I peered over his shoulder and saw a paused video. "Check it out," he said, and pressed the play button. It was a video of our bedroom. I cocked my head, confused. Then I entered the frame and walked across our bedroom toward the bed, and … I was naked. My eyes widened, and my hands involuntarily shot up to cover my eyes. Then I started to peek through my fingers.

"What? What is this? What did you do?"

"What do you mean, what did I do? I recorded us having sex." I glared back with the look that no man ever wants to see from his wife.

"What, you don't like it? I thought you'd like it. You look hot."

"You don't get it. Who does that? What kind of person would do this behind their wife's back?" His tone changed from excitement to apology.

"But, it's so great. It's so hot and you look gorgeous. It's such a turn-on for me. If you'll just watch it, you'll see," he said.

"No. Look, it's not about the video. It's about me not knowing you were doing it. If you had asked me, I might have said yes. But you didn't." I turned away and walked out the door. I didn't speak to him until we picked up our daughter from her grandparents' house, and we definitely didn't have sex for at least a week.

Several weeks later, I sat working at the same computer, home alone for a few hours. A thought floated through my head. *Should I watch it?* But I was still mad, so I didn't want to ask him where it was. I sleuthed around and found it, then went back and forth about whether to watch it or not. Finally, I was ready to press "play." *But, do I really want to do this? Will I look hideous?* I hadn't had any makeup on. My hair had been a wreck. I hadn't known the camera was rolling, so I hadn't tried to suck in my tummy. *Do I really need to see myself naked?* No.

But I was curious enough to press play.

There I was. It's really hard to look at yourself naked on a 22-inch screen. But after about a minute, I thought, *Hmmm, her hair's not too bad ... I'd let that woman babysit my kid ... I'd like to have coffee with her... I think she'd make a good neighbor... She looks sweet.*

Watching this version of myself, I thought, *"Who is that woman with my husband? That's not me."* Every day, I walked out of my door with full makeup and carefully thought-out outfits just to go to the dentist. Had I known I was being recorded, I would have gone into "performance mode" — sucking in my belly, combing my hair, and putting on some makeup. Instead, I just showed up as me and didn't try to be anything else. But this girl on screen, with her messy hair and no makeup ... she seemed free, graceful, and she was just being herself. Without even trying, she looked more confident than I do in my most practiced moments.

"Wait a minute, that *is* me." That was the first time I saw myself the way other people see me. I was able to witness myself in my most genuine state of being. Watching myself, I was struck by how skewed my self-concept was.

I was watching who I really was and learning that *she is* the person I want to be.

Watching yourself naked on video is hard, but being naked with your clothes on, out in the world, is a lot harder.

A few months later, the next time I walked into a conference center ballroom to give a keynote presentation, I carried a piece of that energy and that girl on the screen with me. I was a bit more willing to be more myself, willing to be emotionally naked. I slowly let go of the masks and lowered the walls I had put up. It didn't happen overnight. I continued to let go, little by little, for the next 10 years.

I remembered that the woman in the video wasn't wearing any masks; she wasn't trying to be powerful, inspiring, compassionate, or vulnerable. Yet, somehow, all of those qualities still came through.

When we are with other people, especially people we don't know well, it is easy to switch into your "performance mode." You try to put on your confident face, your business face, your serious face, or whatever face you think is appropriate for the situation. Unfortunately, people usually realize, consciously or subconsciously, that you are wearing a mask of some sort and are less likely to feel a genuine connection with you.

We all try to project personal qualities that we want others to think we have. For example, "I want to be seen as sweet and lovely" or "I want to be seen as smart and capable." We may actually have some of these qualities, but when they're forced and coming from an inauthentic place, our presence is diminished. When you are projecting, the other person senses you are energetically pushing those qualities out in front of you, driven by the fear that quality won't convey if you don't. But when you stop projecting and are just at home in your skin, you reach your authentic self. That's what people connect to.

EXERCISE: UNCONDITIONAL SELF-LOVE

Record your voice and notice what thoughts, feelings, and sensations come up when you listen back to hear the sound of your own voice.

Videotape yourself talking for about three to five minutes about either a short version of your life story or about what you do for a living. Then watch it; witness yourself and note how you feel when watching yourself. Watch it again, making a conscious effort to witness yourself without judgment and to send love and appreciative thoughts to yourself.

Whenever you leave someone a voicemail message, if there is an option at the end to listen to your message before you send it, take that option and do two things:

> - *Use it to practice improving your speaking skills. Notice if your voice sounds strong and articulate; if you'd like to make any changes, choose the option to re-record and listen again*
> - *Practice loving the sound of your own voice. Listen with compassion and admiration and appreciate all of the qualities and personality that comes out on your voice.*

Extreme Self-Acceptance

One of the most effective habits for developing a positive self-concept is called the "Mirror Exercise," a practice I learned from Jack Canfield. Unfortunately, many of us tend toward "negativity dominance," which means that the vast majority of our thoughts are negative, and the majority of those negative thoughts are things we say about ourselves, our abilities, and our ability to succeed and perform. Only when we increase our awareness of our "little voice," then begin to re-program it with more positive and empowering thoughts, can we begin to create positive changes in our thought patterns.

EXERCISE: THE MIRROR

The mirror exercise is a ritual that can be done anytime but doing it just before bed every night is a great way to establish this habit. It offers an opportunity to slow your mind chatter down and feed yourself positive, encouraging, and appreciative thoughts.

Stand in front of a mirror and look straight into your own eyes. Make a conscious effort to maintain eye contact with yourself.

Acknowledge yourself for specific tasks that you accomplished during the day. Recognize any thoughtful actions that you performed toward others, thank yourself for keeping any commitments to others and to yourself and recognize any other attributes, actions or accomplishments that come up for you.

Complete the exercise by telling yourself, "I love you."

For example, at the end of the day, my mirror exercise dialogue might sound like this:

"Hi, Michelle. I am proud of you for waking up early today to work out even though you were tired. You stayed committed to your health and wellness goals. You didn't get flustered when the road construction caused a traffic jam. You ate a healthy breakfast and you didn't beat yourself up for eating ice cream yesterday. You were productive, finishing your article, responding to e-mails, and following up with three potential clients. You made that phone call even though it was scary. You stayed positive even when you discovered that your e-mails from last week got lost, you made that sales call even thought you were nervous, you made a healthy food choice at lunch and you even cleaned out your car. I'm proud of you and I love you. You expressed your appreciation for two of your employees, which made them feel good and made you feel good. You made time to read with your daughter before bed. You are responsible, and you are a good wife and mother. I love you. Goodnight."

As you are acknowledging yourself, you can include the following:

- *Any achievements, including business, financial, educational, personal, physical, spiritual, or emotional.*
- *Any personal disciplines you kept, including dietary, exercise, reading, meditation, or prayer habits.*
- *Any temptations that you did not give in to, such as eating dessert, lying, watching too much TV, staying up too late, or drinking too much.*

It's not unusual to feel silly, embarrassed, emotional, or just generally uncomfortable. Hang in there. It gets more fun the more often you do it -- and you deserve it!

Some people find they can't hold eye contact with themselves; some have a hard time generating a list if they're not used to appreciating their own efforts. Many don't say the "I love you" with meaning, perhaps looking away, rolling their eyes, or slurring or glazing over the words quickly.

Whatever happens or comes up is perfect. Simply keep at it until you feel the love. Eventually, if you haven't already, you will fall in love with yourself. The most highly successful, confident, and happy people truly have a love affair with themselves. I don't mean they're cocky or arrogant; they simply hold themselves in the highest regard.

When you do, two very important things become possible. 1) You create the space to allow others to hold you in high regard. 2) You open yourself up enough to hold others in high regard, valuing them and their efforts and enabling you to express to them how loved and valuable they are.

When you are able to express these things to yourself, you will naturally become a master at letting other people know how valuable and loved they are, even sometimes without saying a word.

EXERCISE: BODY APPRECIATION

Just as you're learning to love your spirit body and all your traits and parts of your personality, this particular mirror exercise involves appreciating and loving your physical body. Whenever possible, it is ideal to do this completely naked.

Stand facing yourself in front of the mirror, preferably a full-length mirror if possible and simply "be with" yourself, breathing deeply, and practicing accepting yourself — all parts

> *of yourself, unconditionally. Take in all parts of your physical self and notice what comes up for you in terms of judgments. Then practice letting them go. See yourself as perfect and complete. (This exercise is best done naked.)*
>
> *Thank your unique body for all the things that it does for you. Maybe you can acknowledge your smile for lighting up your face when you're happy. Maybe you can acknowledge your heart for circulating blood throughout your body without you having to think of it. Or you can acknowledge your hands and fingers for allowing you to speak to others, brush your teeth, caress your loved ones, paint, or write. Perhaps you can thank your hair for framing your face. Thank any other parts that occur to you to acknowledge.*
>
> *Pay special love and attention to those parts of you and your body you may not like or have wanted to change. Tell them that you're sorry, that you love them, and that you will show it by thinking positive thoughts about them in the future.*
>
> *Do this mirror exercise for at least five minutes each day for five days. See what happens. You can also practice doing this by picking one thing about yourself to acknowledge and appreciate every time you walk by a mirror. Put post-it notes on your mirrors to remind you.*

In a world where there is so much temptation to put on a brave face and project confidence, it is easy to fall into the habit of presenting to the world only the parts of us we are proud of or that we want people to see. But when we do that, we create an invisible wall that prevents people from seeing our real selves. If nobody can see who we really are, they can never really love, accept, and connect with us in the way our souls crave. It is only when we are willing to show up emotionally naked that we can create the kinds of connections and understanding that will leave a lasting imprint on people. Those who are willing to shed the armor, take off the masks, and be unapologetically human have the best possibility of communicating with power and compassion and inspiring change and transformation.

When you combine the fierceness of your Hara energy with an open, compassionate heart, you will show up in the world in a way that cannot be ignored. And when you add the energy of divine consciousness connected with the next energy center that we are going to explore, you will be an unstoppable force.

HEAD

Connect With Your Head-Centered Energy
for Maximum Impact and Influence

CHAPTER 9

Your Gateway to Higher Consciousness

Embodying Your Head Space

Now that we've stoked the fire of our pleasure power center and cleared our heart channel, it's time to return to our head center with new energy and intention.

Most of us associate "being in your head" with a state where we are focused on distracting thoughts, worries, concerns, analyzing and overanalyzing, and spending time thinking to the exclusion of feeling. But when you are in that very "mental" state, you are not really "in your head," because your awareness and energy are not focused physically on the space inside your head. Instead, you are dissociated with your physical body, including your head, brain, skull, and face.

Activating our true energy center in our head, both physically and energetically, is equally as important as the other two. Your Upper Dantien is associated with your higher chakras, which in turn are related to your ability to access intuition, "God" or Universal energy, connection with your Higher Self, and are also key to integrating, transmuting, and making the best use of the energy you generate in your Hara or Pleasure Power Center. Achieving the "Sweet Spot" requires presence and activation in all three centers — it allows you to radiate a powerful presence and magnetism.

You will start to experience that truly being in your head feels fantastic.

Follow Your Heart, But Take Your Head With You

Many "left brain" people (including me) are used to making decisions and leading from our heads versus our hearts. We've tried to rely solely on intellect, reason, and pros and cons. For us, a big part of this work is to learn to lead with the heart, but not to leave the head behind. Our brains are powerful; our intuition and "head-centered" energy can serve us as we passionately follow our hearts and lead with passion and purpose. Ideally, we can take our thoughts out of the driver's seat, not leave them on the side of the road.

Being stuck in your head is what most people describe as focusing on the busy thoughts in your mind. But truly being present in your head is desirable, and much different from being in your head bubble. Just as we have practiced feeling sensation in our pleasure power centers, in our hands, in our hearts and throughout our bodies, we also want to practice feeling heightened sensation in our brains, eyes, nose, mouth, tongue, ears, and entire heads.

EXERCISE: HEAD TAPPING

We've learned whole-body tapping and chest tapping; now, it's time to focus on tapping the top of the head, forehead, between the eyebrows, cheeks, the bones under your eyes, up and down the jaw, lightly across the front of the neck, firmly across the back of the neck, and all over the back of the head, especially the spot on the back of your head where the base of your skull and the top of your neck meet.

Listen to what feels good to you and pay more attention to the spots that are calling for more attention. Some days it may feel good to spend most of your time tapping the point between your eyebrows, and some days you may want to spend all your time tapping the top of your head.

When you begin to sensitize your head, you will notice how good it feels to be present in this important energy center within your body. This is one of three key elements to achieving the "sweet spot."

EXERCISE: OCCUPYING YOUR UPPER ENERGY CENTER

Begin by gently closing your eyes and becoming aware of your breathing and the temperature of your body. Focus on the feelings in your mouth and in your tongue. Notice if your mouth feels dry, if there is a significant amount of saliva present, or if it's somewhere in between. Notice if any distracting thoughts are running through your head. If there are, simply tell them you'll be back to pay attention to them later, but that they can take a break and go relax for the moment.

Become aware of your nose, the feeling of air entering and exiting though your nostrils. Notice if you can sense any lingering tastes in your mouth.

Be In Your Head, Not In Your Head Bubble

Play the game of catching yourself when you are not occupying the space within or fully embodying your head. Here are some clues that you are probably not embodying your head:

- You catch yourself looking up at the ceiling or at the sky or into space

- Feeling like your head is in the clouds

- Gazing down at the floor

- Feeling like you searching outside of yourself for answers

- Unable to hold eye contact during conversations

- Talking too fast

- Talking too slow

- Feeling hot or flushed in your face

When you are not occupying the space in your head, you will feel as if your thoughts are floating above you. You may also feel like your eyes are staring off into the distance rather than being fully present to what is right in front of you. You can use your eye-gaze to help you gauge how present and embodied you are in your head. Many times, an upward or downward gaze indicates that you are in your head-bubble and therefore not embodied in your head.

When you catch yourself in your "head bubble," that imaginary space above and outside your head, take a few moments to focus on your breath, the temperature of your body, and connect to your power center. Re-center yourself and consciously bring all of your energy and attention inside your own body until you feel grounded and fully aware of your own skin, your vibration, and the quality of the energy circulating throughout your body.

One of the differences between being in your head bubble and being present in your body is the ability to observe your thoughts, rather than letting them run the show.

The Power of "Feeling" Affirmations

At the beginning of this book, I said that affirmations are overrated. In my experience, you can recite positive affirmations and never feel different or produce different results. In order for affirmations or the law of attraction to work, the statements must be accompanied by feelings, such as the whole-body sensations we practiced in Part One. Getting used to tuning into your life-force energy will help you turn your affirmations into "feeling affirmations." We can use our brains and ability to choose our thoughts to create statements that reflect our desires, and we can use our ability to generate sensation and energy vibrations to turbo-charge those affirmations and make them more effective.

The law of attraction is based on the ability of energy to act as an attractor, not on the ability of thoughts to act as an attractor. But the energy can be assisted by our thoughts and intention — when we learn to use our brains properly and clear our minds of unnecessary clutter, we are better positioned to use our three main energy centers in unison.

EXERCISE: ACTIVATE YOUR UPPER ENERGY CENTER

Close your eyes and focus on the sound of your own breath. Continue to breathe naturally as you start to bring your attention and energy to your face, head, skull, eyes, and brain. Imagine a point of light energy located in the approximate center of your head. See and feel it living and breathing with you. Use this point of light as your anchor. It will help keep you in your vibrant head center rather than your head bubble.

In Part One, you practiced becoming more sensitized to your body and your energy. You began by sensing the energy in your hands and then progressed to feeling your energy vibration in your arms, legs, torso, and the rest of your body.

Interestingly, I have found that when I ask clients and workshop participants to feel the life-force energy coursing through and radiating off their bodies, they usually don't include their heads. Many people are unaccustomed to paying attention to the sensations they feel in their heads, especially pleasurable sensations. For example, most people would find it much easier to gently move their hips or shoulders in a pleasurable way than to move their heads in a pleasurable way.

Now, take those energy connection skills you've developed and apply the same principles toward increasing awareness and sensation in your head energy center.

Begin by rubbing your hands together to begin to connect with your energy. As you slowly pull them apart, sense the energy that is not only in your hands, but that is radiating off your hands. When you're ready to move on, slowly bring your awareness of your internal energy and radiating presence up your arms, into your torso, and into your legs and your feet. See if you can feel the energy in each toe.

Now that you're warmed up, try feeling the energy in your head and in your brain.

As you do this practice, periodically close your eyes in between reading this section.

What do you notice?

Does it feel light?

Does it feel heavy?

Buzzing with energy?

Cool?

Clear?

Hot?

Dull sensations?

Discomfort or pain?

Bring your awareness to your eyeballs and eye sockets. How do they feel?

Shift your focus to your nose. Does it feel open? Stuffy? Clear? What else?

Now, bring your attention to your mouth and your tongue. Do you have a lot or a little saliva in your mouth? Can you feel the energy in the tip of your tongue? How about the back of your mouth and throat?

Now, focus on the left hemisphere of your brain. Put all of your attention on feeling sensation in it.

Next, focus on feeling the right hemisphere of your brain.

Don't worry if you start to feel slight aches or pains. This practice might seem to cause unpleasant sensations if you have been going on about your life unaware that there are energy blockages and pain points in this part of your body. As you practice getting quiet and still and focusing on your own energy, you will begin to notice things you have been overlooking, living with, or have come to accept as your normal state of being.

With your eyes closed, breathe in and out, imaging that all the heavy, stagnant, negative energy is escaping from your head through your exhalations.

Once you have finished sensing the various parts of your head, return your attention to the key energy point in your head energy center: the space between your eyebrows and in the middle of your head. Just as you have learned to focus on a sphere of light living and breathing in the center of your pelvis, imagine a small sphere of light energy in the center of your head at the level of your eyebrows.

Just as focusing on the center of your pelvis can help you feel grounded, focusing on the center of your head can help you feel mentally balanced.

Embodying your head by maintaining focus on this point can be an important tool for staying present and out of your head bubble, whether by yourself or in conversation.

EXERCISE: THIRD-EYE GAZING PRACTICE

Gently close your eyes and begin focusing on the feeling of air entering in and exiting out of your nose as you breathe. Notice if it feels cool or warm as it passes through your nostrils.

Now focus on your eyeballs and with your eyes still closed, look at the space between your eyes, creating a cross-eyed inner gaze as you look at this third eye energetic space. This practice will help you achieve better mental clarity and inner knowing.

EXERCISE: BRAIN BALANCING PRACTICE

Most people are either left-brain or right-brain dominant. You can perform at your peak ability when both sides of your brain are in harmony and are communicating with one another, when you've incorporated both your logical, practical, reasoning brain with your intuitive, creative brain.

You can balance the two hemispheres of your brain using your focused attention and a simple harmonizing practice you can do anywhere.

Begin by relaxing into a comfortable sitting position. Begin to focus on the energy circulating throughout your body. Bring all of your attention into your body, telling any distracting thoughts that you will be back later to pay attention to them; put them into an imaginary parking lot.

Focus on feeling sensation in and putting all of your attention on the right hemisphere of your brain for a few moments. Notice if you feel any type of sensation, for example, buzzing, vibration, aching, pain, pulsating.

Then, switch all of your energy and attention to the left hemisphere of your brain for a few moments.

Now, imagine that there is an infinity symbol made of moving light particles that is sitting in your brain horizontally, connecting both hemispheres of your brain. Visualize the light-powered infinity symbol circulating and connecting energy between the two sides of your brain.

For a moment, allow the light and movement to circulate at a pace that feels comfortable to you. Then stop and notice how you feel in your body. Resume the practice for one additional minute and then allow yourself to sit in stillness, allowing your body and brain time to integrate the benefits of this practice.

With continued practice, you will feel more balanced in your brain and in your overall energy, able to engage and utilize both parts of your brain for maximum effectiveness.

The increased sensation you will begin to develop will help you stay centered in your head, allowing you to project a more powerful presence.

EXERCISE: PRACTICE ALTERNATE NOSTRIL BREATHING

Alternate nostril is a type of yogic breathing that provides an effective method for balancing your nervous system and the hemispheres of your brain. Begin by using your thumb to close off your right nostril as you inhale solely through your left nostril. Then, release your thumb and close off your left nostril with your index finger of the same hand as you exhale through your right nostril. Then inhale through your right nostril. Continue switching breathing in and out of each nostril for one breath cycle, alternating after each inhalation.

You can also achieve specific effects with this breathing, depending on which nostril you breathe through. In circumstances where stress levels are high and I need to relax, I breathe solely in and out through the left nostril, because breathing through the left side of the nose calms the system. Right-nostril breathing, on the other hand, is useful when you want to increase your energy levels. So, depending on how you're feeling, you can choose which one to use.

EXERCISE: VERTICAL CORE

In previous chapters, you practiced staying connected to your power center, your heart center, and your head center individually. We have been building up to being able to put all of your attention and energy on all three of these points at the same time.

First, practice with your eyes closed. Begin by seeing and feeling the point of light energy in your pleasure power center. Once it's clear and resonant, add in the sensation and focus on feeling and imagining the point of light energy in the center of your heart space. Finally, put your attention on the light energy in your head. Practice holding your attention on all three points at the same time. Notice what it feels like to be present in all three energy centers at once. Imagine there is an invisible cord connecting these three points. Enjoy this feeling for at least one full minute before moving on to the next step.

Next, try holding your attention and energy in the center of your head, heart, and Hara all at the same time with your eyes open. Adding in visual stimulation will make this a bit more challenging. Next, work your way up to maintaining this focus and connection of all three points while you are walking and talking and interacting with people. This takes practice, but when you are able to sustain this state of being, you will feel stronger, more connected, more powerful, magnetic, and articulate. You may notice that you are standing and sitting up taller, your spine feels straighter, your posture is improved, and you have increased range of motion and a heightened sense of alertness. You may also feel that your body parts are more in sync, as if your whole body is now moving in unison and cooperating as a complete unit rather than disparate parts in opposition to each other. Being in this state will also help protect you from having people invade your energetic space, and will keep you from inadvertently entering others' energetic spaces.

The more aware you are of your head, the more you can contain your energy because many people tend to let their precious energy escape through their heads. To keep your vital life-force energy contained within your body, you can practice putting one or two hands firmly on top of your head and imagine that in doing this, you are putting on an invisible cap.

> *Then once you remove your hands, see if you can maintain that sensation of having a crown or cap of energetic protection to contain your energy.*

One of the key indicators that you are successfully embodying and using all three key energy centers (Head, Heart, and Hara) is that you feel as if your body parts are moving together as a unit. When I learned this skill, I noticed that even talking feels different depending on whether or not I am embodying my head.

I've had the privilege of working with Jean-Louis Rodrigue, a movement coach who works with world-famous actors and speakers to help them communicate with their physicality. During one of his training sessions I learned to speak from the back of my head.

I began this exercise by using my fingertips to tap the top, back, and sides of my head, including my forehead, jaw, and occipital bone, at the base of my head where it meets my neck. Jean-Louis emphasized how important it is to activate this area, because it is near our optic nerve. We tend to think that we see through our eyes, but Jean-Louis pointed out that we actually see images through our optic nerve. This understanding of my vision helps me connect not just to the front of my face but to my entire brain and head space.

After I tapped, I practiced saying my name out loud several times while focusing on originating the sound from the back of my head. Interestingly, I noticed a big difference in the way I felt and the way I sounded. I felt stronger, more connected to power, and my voice itself felt and sounded more powerful and resonant.

Try tapping the back of your head for about a minute. Pause. Notice that even after you stop tapping you can still sense energy there, almost pulsating. This is your energetic presence that we've been connecting to with our hands and other body parts. Now say your name out loud several times and take note of how you feel and what you sound like.

A Clear Head Leads to a Clear Energy Channel

In Part Three of this book, you will practice circulating energy between your three main energy centers (Head, Heart and Hara). The exercises in this chapter will help ensure that you are equipped with the tools and awareness to enjoy the benefits of having life-force energy flow throughout your body, invigorating and healing it in the process. You will also be more likely to allow vital energy from the Universe to enter your body through the crown of your head to bring in new, fresh energy, ideas, and inspiration.

Having a clear, cool head is also crucial in the upcoming energy-circulating exercises because most of us are at risk of collecting too much energy in our head centers, due to our tendency to overthink and the fact that we engage heavily in mental tasks throughout the day. Learning to clear and embody your head will help ensure that the energy you circulate into your head won't get stuck there. Ideally, you've cleared enough blockages to allow the energy to make a complete loop back to your pleasure power center after cleansing your brain and your head. Collecting energy in your pleasure power center has many benefits, but collecting and storing energy in your head can cause an energetic imbalance.

By practicing the embodiment and relaxation techniques we've covered so far, your brain and head should become more clear and quiet. It is in this state that we can best use the power of our minds to assist us in thinking, feeling, and being confident and magnetic. Developing the ability to notice, accept, or reject the thoughts that cross our minds helps us notice and even intensify the energy behind the positive thoughts. Our brains need to be involved in this process of reprogramming our entire being to radiate high vibrations.

PART THREE

Achieving the Sweet Spot

CHAPTER 10

Your Primal Nature

Strong Physical Presence

Just like the athlete who enters the field, court, or arena, animals are on high alert. They have to be fully present. You don't see animals walking across the Serengeti desert slouching or unaware. They are in tune with their surroundings and walk with calm alertness. Their whole bodies are expressive, and when you see them in action, you can't take your eyes off them. The same is true for us. If we are fully embodied and fully expressive, people will not be able to take their eyes off us.

Embodiment is why musicians, athletes, dancers, singers, and performers captivate us so powerfully. In order to pursue these activities, you must be totally present in your body if you want to be any good. Imagine a professional basketball player who is primarily in her head during the big championship game. Distraction and second-guessing would probably lead her to move slower and potentially even get injured — when you're in your head, you're disconnected from your instincts, and if you're disconnected from your instincts, your reactions will be too slow for a fast-paced game. The same is true for a dancer: if he is too busy thinking about which moves come next, the performance will be choppy instead of seamless and embodied. Orators, too: the best speakers in the world are fully present when they take the stage. They know it's not just about giving a speech; it's about delivering a performance. People in these situations entrance their viewers because full presence is such a rare experience in our society.

But these high performers' ability to engage at 100% in their chosen endeavors doesn't automatically transfer off-stage or off-court. Have you ever seen a performer — maybe a talented pro basketball player or a favorite actor — in an interview, and the conversation just falls flat? You wonder if this is the same person: how could they be so amazing on the court or on screen and then be so uninteresting as they talk to the interviewer? Often, they don't apply the same high-performance practices to situations outside their expertise. It's not deliberate; it just doesn't occur to them to do the same for media interviews, meet-and-greets, and in their normal, everyday life. They might also hold the common belief that they need to save this special focus for game time, but that's not true. In fact, most would probably say that after entering the zone, they stay energized, even for hours or days after the game, because it actually fills them up and energizes them. If they applied the same principles to play in the game of life this way, they would experience even more energy and aliveness.

Most of us don't earn our living playing in these zones, which makes it even more important to treat every day like game time and to treat every room we enter like our stage if we want to stand out, produce amazing work, be recognized, and feel fulfilled.

I see a similar phenomenon after yoga and meditation classes. I am a huge fan of meditation, it is a great tool for coming back to ourselves and connecting with our true nature. But what I see in so many people is that while they are able to achieve a calm, centered, powerful state during their meditations, the results don't always last as long as they would like them to. At my yoga studio, many people walk in frazzled, distracted, and off-center, but as soon as they enter the yoga room, it's like walking into a parallel universe. By taking just one step over the threshold into the practice room, they are instantly transported into a familiar state. The room is associated with feelings of calm and groundedness; this is the place where they commit to focusing on nothing but themselves and their practice.

But then an odd yet unfortunate thing happens. Many of the women I see in the locker room after class return to their hurried, disconnected, overthinking states. They enjoy this wonderful experience but have a hard time remaining in that clear, centered, body-connected state. Or perhaps they don't make a conscious choice to want to stay in that place. They may hold an unconscious belief that the time to enjoy that state is during the 60- or 75-minute practice, not after the class ends.

Embodiment is not only for sports, performances, and physical activity. This is the secret that all great inspirational leaders and exceptional communicators know. They know that if they stay as present as an elite athlete does, people will not be able to look away from them. They know that if they embrace their divine nature and primal power and instincts, that they will exude a powerful presence.

How Do You Apologize With Your Body?

Having a powerful and magnetic presence and achieving your energetic sweet spot, aka your "E Spot," as my mentor refers to it, requires a heightened awareness of how you hold yourself when you are fully present in your body while exuding your juicy life-force energy. You cannot achieve your sweet spot if you are not aware of how you tend to apologize with your body.

Your body language speaks louder than your words. If your body says you are unsure, hesitant, self-conscious, or otherwise lacking in confidence, people will pick up on that immediately, even if only subconsciously, and no amount of brilliant words will change their perception.

You may recognize in yourself some of these common traits and behaviors that people exhibit when they apologize with their bodies:

- Clasping their hands in front of their bodies (sometimes referred to as the fig-leaf pose). This is sometimes a subconscious attempt to cover up the private parts, because they can sometimes make us feel vulnerable when they are unguarded.

- Clasping hands behind their back (reverse fig-leaf pose)

- Rocking back and forth with your body

- Swaying your body side to side

- Keeping your hands in your pockets

- Playing with your hair or your keys or change in your pockets

- Looking up at the ceiling while talking

- Looking down at the ground while talking

- Shoulders caving in

- Hanging head down

- Tilting of the head

- Slouching

- Speaking too softly

Conversely, here are some ways in which we demonstrate that we are physically and energetically standing strong and in our power:

- Feet about hip-width apart and solidly planted on the ground

- Standing or sitting up straight

- Head held high

- Maintaining eye contact

- Speaking with a strong, articulate voice

EXERCISE: OWNING YOUR POWER VERSUS APOLOGIZING FOR YOUR POWER

Pretend you are introducing yourself to a stranger. The first time you do it, purposely apologize with your body while you speak. Purposely exhibit some of the behaviors and postures listed above: looking down, hunching your shoulders, or swaying your body to indicate instability. Take a mental note of what this feels like in your body and what it does to your mental state and to your ability to communicate.

Try this a second time, but before you begin, practice getting grounded in your feet first. I like to stomp on the ground several times with each foot as if I'm about to perform The Lord of the Dance. I find this gets me into my body.

> *Return to a regular standing posture and recall what it feels like to be aware of your energetic presence and adjust your posture to make sure that you are physically standing in your power, arms comfortably at your sides and not apologizing with your body. Then re-introduce yourself.*
>
> *You may also want to try waking up your physical body by engaging a high-squat position for about 20 seconds, as if you're huddling up with a football team before the next play. The action of getting into a semi-squat engages the lower part of your body and helps fire up the area in and around your power center.*
>
> *Notice the differences between how you felt the first time versus how you felt the second time.*

Powered By Glutes

Right before my fellow trainees and I were about to get on stage during speech rehearsals, one of my speaking coaches asked us to get into a huddle, as he used to do with his team when he played professional football. Squatting down and activating those glute muscles helped us activate our power, our solid foundation, and the ability to move onstage with a powerful presence. It helped us get into our bodies.

Tantra also emphasizes the importance of doing squats and strengthening this part of your body that supports you and gives you a strong foundation. European beauty standards often value a slim figure and lean gluteus muscles, but, really, we should be building that thing up! Squats and other glute-building exercises send energy to your lower chakras, which can be so easy to ignore if you're always in your head. If your legs, buttocks, and core are strong, you will feel safer, and more grounded and powerful. You will feel you have a strong foundation, a sensation that translates energetically, too.

When you feel strong, safe, and grounded, you will feel like you can handle more and will be more likely to take healthy risks because of your solid foundation. When you stand strong in the lower part of your body, you give the rest of your system permission to go out and play and express itself.

What might be possible if we applied ourselves and experience what it's like to operate at full capacity? Most of us are afraid to go 100%; we worry we'll overdo it, we'll blow a gasket, or that engagement level just feels completely foreign and unnatural to us because we are used to watering ourselves down or holding back. Maybe we want to conserve our energy, maybe we don't want to draw attention to ourselves, maybe we're worried about overwhelming other people. Or we might worry that if we go full out once, we won't be able to duplicate that effort, and it will have just been a fluke, a stroke of good luck. Whatever the reason, we operate at 50% capacity (or less) because we're in the habit of saving up our energy or potential for the "perfect" time to use it.

Performing at 100% capacity doesn't have to feel like hard work; in fact, if you're trying too hard, the output is unsustainable and will exhaust you instead of inspiring and energizing you. Instead of pushing, you can release the brakes on your potential and let yourself be unleashed. Being unleashed is very different from trying — it's about allowing yourself to release your energy and operate at full capacity.

Say "Yes" to Embracing Your Full Capacity

I experienced what operating and being in the energetic state of 100% feels like during an energetic yoga training session. It was less about yoga poses and more about energetics and embodiment. The facilitator introduced us to a game in which, one by one, each participant crossed the room in a creative way. The only rule was that when you crossed, you had to do it in a way distinct from what all the others had done before you. For example, you could crawl, skip, roll, hop, etc. Some participants were giggling, letting loose, and enjoying themselves, and some were putting on a brave face even though it seemed like they were far out of their comfort zones. Initially, I was somewhere in the middle.

Once our energy and creativity was engaged, the teacher introduced a new facet of the exercise: we had to cross the room in an energetic state that was as close to 100% as we could get — using total energy, body, voice, and enthusiasm. The goal was to demonstrate that you were channeling as much of your energy as possible, not a watered-down version of yourself. Our only instructions were to cross the room any way we chose, as long as it was a fully self-expressed form that told the world we meant business. She asked us to energetically tell the world we have arrived, and that we believe in ourselves and our abilities.

One at a time, we crossed the room in random order, with the freedom to step up when we felt it was our turn to go. I didn't want to go first or last, so I was in the first third of people to cross. One woman did a bear crawl while making roaring noises and one man walked across on his hands announcing his name along the way. The energy became more and more electric and contagious. Most people were loud when they crossed, but our teacher wasn't looking just for volume and big expression — she looked into our eyes to see if she really believed us. Just making a loud noise and flailing your limbs around was not the goal. She wanted to see intensity and power behind our movement.

Five years earlier, this kind of exercise would have freaked me out. But now, I was at a place in my life where I was comfortable with self-expression and more used to letting my intuition guide me. I stayed present to the experience of witnessing the other participants. Then, when it was my turn, I surrendered to the exercise, following the first idea that came to me — the Yes breath.

I'd learned the Yes breath from my Tantra teacher. You raise both hands up straight into the air, look up to the sky, and then bend your elbows and pull both arms back to hit the sides of your body as you say, "Yes." You say "yes" over and over again, saying yes to the Universe and everything it has to offer you, saying yes to everything you want and desire, saying yes to all of your goals, dreams, intentions, and saying yes to your potential and to loving yourself and loving life.

I'd been practicing the Yes Breath for a year, standing or sitting still, and I thought I'd been doing it right, but in the yoga workshop, as I took my first step across the room, I realized that I had been well below my energetic 100% capacity.

So right there in that room with its yellow rubber floor, I decided to give it my 100% effort. I didn't care if I looked silly. I decided to let go of all my thoughts about the right thing to do and allowed all my energy and power to come through. I allowed my instincts to take over. It felt a little bit like an out-of-body experience, like my body was moving faster than I could think, which was new and good. I didn't have time to overthink what I should do, so I just threw myself into the center of the room and allowed my mouth and body to take me where they wanted to take me.

I began to move my Yes Breath across the room. I shouted "yes!" louder than I ever had before, my voice soaring from a place deep inside my belly, a place of resonance, commitment, and depth. I was expending more energy than I had in a long time, yet doing so made me feel more energized.

After I stopped, I actually felt like it had fueled me. And in that moment, for a second, flashbacks and regret flooded my mind — what might my life have been like if I had been willing to go to 100% sooner? What more could I have accomplished? How much happier and successful would I be? But I didn't dwell in that place for long. I quickly just reveled in this feeling and started to wonder, could I do this all the time?

When I left the workshop, I did something out of character for me. I hopped into my car, picked up my phone, and made a call to a prospective client. This may not sound like a big deal to some, but for me, it was. As an extreme introvert, my preference is almost always to correspond via e-mail or text if possible. On the rare occasions when I am going to make a phone call, I don't like to multi-task by talking while driving — I prefer to sit at my desk with a list of prepared questions and discussion items and a notepad to take notes. Unscripted, unplanned real-time conversations have not always been my preference.

When he picked up and we started talking, it first felt like I was speaking loudly, but then I realized that my voice was just stronger and I wasn't used to feeling the power behind it. Something as simple as a phone call, taking immediate action, and trusting that I would know the right things to say without thinking about my plan of attack taught me the intensity of my own power and how I had been limiting myself.

The Yes Breath

The Yes Breath is designed to help you increase your energy, awaken your senses, and stimulate your primal power. You raise both arms into the air and then quickly bring them back down as you bend your elbows and bring your elbows back in to the sides of your body near your waistline and you shout "yes" as you do it each time. You do this repeatedly for at least two minutes straight to get the energy and blood flow. When you try this, don't be afraid to hit the sides of your body with your arms and elbows with a good amount of force. Doing so will help wake up and shake up your body. While I'm doing it, I like to do it with the intention that as I say "Yes!" I am saying yes to all the blessings and all the abundance that the universe has to offer. I am saying "yes" to life, "yes" to realizing my goals and dreams, "yes" to being energized, awake, sensual, alive, and powerful.

100%, All The Time

Most of us don't use our bodies and our voices as much as we should. We were given voices; we need to use them. We need to sing and shout and let it all out. Children are so good at this, but as we get older we tend to become more reserved. All of the expression that we hold in gets bottled-up and makes our bodies tense and our energy blocked. We need to move and be wild, dance, skip, play, use our body to move and our expressions to communicate. Do you know what it's like to go all out? To give it your all? What if you approached life with the intention of doing everything full out? Putting all your energy and effort into every conversation, every phone call, every project, every chore, every walk, every workout. Remember, going all out doesn't mean running at your day naked and screaming wildly — it can mean simply focusing your entire attention on helping your daughter with her math homework, or being fully aware of the sound of the water splashing in the sink as you do the dishes after dinner.

At 100%, you are using your entire body to do the activity you are doing. Your entire body is involved. Every muscle, every fiber, every cell, every body part is involved. Part of why this exercise and experience of full-body involvement feels so good and has a lasting effect is because when you are engaged in every part of your physical and energetic body, you have no choice but to be fully present. If you are able to multi-task, then you are not doing it right.

Because, when you are at 100%, you are fully engaged and all of your attention is on what it right in front of you. This is an exhilarating, but sadly uncommon, occurrence for most. We are so used to multi-tasking and "watering ourselves down" in an effort to conserve our energy, not appear too confident, not make anyone feel inferior, not make any waves.

Does this mean that I am suggesting that you shout and be overly animated in everything that you do? No, of course not. The exercise is to feel the feeling of what 100% capacity feels like in your body but once you practice it, you can embody 100% presence no matter how loud or silent you are. With practice, you'll be able to arrive at that state while controlling it, containing it, and directing it as the situation calls for.

Hysterical Strength

Sometimes your potential comes out when you feel called to defend or protect a loved one. Lauren Kornacki was 22 years old when she lifted a BMW off her dad, who had been pinned underneath the car while trying to fix a blown tire. There are numerous other accounts of "hysterical strength" where people somehow summon super-human strength in life-or-death situations.

Sometimes, the strength isn't physical, but is instead uncharacteristic courage, emotional strength, or vocal power.

One day, my family and I were walking around the historic plaza in downtown Santa Fe, NM, making our way toward a coffee shop. The sidewalks were crowded with people who were there for a special event. Outside the coffee shop, a scowling, angry woman yelled at my mom to be more careful. Apparently, she'd been offended that my mom's purse had touched the side of her arm. My mom froze, shocked by this woman's disproportionate intensity and expression. Without thinking, I stepped between my mom and the woman, pointed my finger close to her face, and barked, "You don't talk to her; you talk to me." The woman looked surprised as if she didn't expect that someone was going to pop up seemingly out of nowhere to defend the woman she was trying to bully. I think we were all a little surprised that I had stepped up to defend my mom without hesitation. After the initial shock of having an unpleasant encounter on our family outing, we sat down and had some good laughs about my alter ego that tends to show up when the situation calls for it. Now there is a running joke in my family; when someone gets mad at someone and gets in their face, they reply with the phrase, "You don't talk to her; you talk to me."

If you mess with my mama, you may see another side of me. (This same version of me showed up when I confronted the woman who made my little sister cry on the day of her baby shower.) At first, I just thought it was funny. But, now I realize I'm not ashamed of that side of me. It's nothing to apologize for — it brings courage, strength, and passion; those are all things I can always use more of.

That warrior spirit lives in all of us and with practice, we can summon it at will. We can use the same methods of muscle memory and use the power of active visualization to enter this state of being.

Think of the last time you stood up for something or someone. Recall what that felt like in your body: feel the adrenaline, feel the lack of fear. Imagine how useful it could be to approach your days and your tasks with that same raw, passionate, fearless energy. You can use it to promote yourself, make sales calls, build something, or convince people to support an important idea or concept that can improve lives.

It is impossible to achieve greatness if you simply try to do something. (Yoda was right: "Do. Or do not. There is no try.") Right now, look around you and find a pen or other small object. Lift it into the air. Set it back down.

Now, demonstrate what it would look like if you were showing someone what it looks like to "try" to lift it up in the air. You might find yourself slowly and awkwardly lifting a pen, or fumbling with a coin, never quite getting it up high. Something similar happens in our bodies and our brains when we "try" to do something, even when it is not something physical. There is struggle; there is a lack of ease. If we decide that we are only going to try to do something, it messes with our ability to just do it without thinking.

Animal Embodiment

In my Art of Feminine Presence teachings, I teach a practice that entails embodying three types of animals: a snake, an eagle and a wildcat. I've led groups of women through the practice of closing their eyes and visualizing becoming and embodying these three animals. I have had my mentor lead me through the same closed-eye exercise.

However, the most powerful experience I've had with this exercise was with a movement and stage-presence coach who works with Hollywood stars.

He introduced the familiar exercise similar to the way I do, but then he added something that made a significant difference — he had us actually walk or crawl or move like the animal that we chose to embody. Instead of just closing our eyes and imagining that we were cats, we actually got down on all fours and practiced moving that way. I chose to be a king cobra, so I lay on the ground and slithered with my cobra head up, imagining my dark, shiny, black cobra hood over my head.

All my abstract notions about cobras became viscerally real. I loved having more than 75% of my body in connection with the earth. The color black signified strength to me and made me feel fierce, the broad hood around my face made me feel regal, and slithering around invoked my sensuality — all together, embodying the cobra made me feel powerful, mysterious, and sexy.

Then he had us start to stand up very slowly. Once we were fully standing, he asked us to hold the intention of being 50% human and 50% animal, then 75% human and 25% animal. It was a smooth transition into walking and talking normally while keeping alive the energy introduced by the animal embodiment. My feet felt more connected to the earth than ever, and I felt strong yet flexible in the rest of my body, the cobra's slithery energy still flowing through me. Before that moment, I felt I could be either strong or sensual, but when I embodied the cobra, I channeled both simultaneously. I realized that strong didn't have to equal stiff.

EXERCISE: CHANNEL YOUR INNER ANIMAL

If you had to pick one animal to embody right now, what would it be?

Close your eyes and ask yourself what animal has an energy you are drawn to.

Take some nice, natural breaths and activate your power center. Begin to pay attention to the life-force energy circulating through your body.

Begin to allow yourself to go into the shape of the animal you have chosen.

If you have chosen a four-legged creature, you can get down on your knees; if you are a bird, you may want to stay on your legs and spread your arms out like wings. If you're a snake, you can put most of your body on the ground with the exception of your head, possibly.

Look around through the eyes of your animal. Engage your senses. Move as your animal would. Put yourself completely into the character of this animal as best you can. Allow yourself to experience the world through the perspective of this animal.

Now start to make the sound of your chosen animal.

Notice what feels different in terms of your breathing, your mental state, your alertness.

As you transition to your "normal" or upright posture, transition with the intention of retaining at least twenty-five percent of the primal qualities of your animal.

Experiment with several different animals. Everyone can benefit from embodying a powerful cat, like a lion, tiger, or cheetah. One of the most helpful aspects of cat embodiment is attention to the tail because it can provide incredible grounding. I like to imagine my long, thick tail grazing the ground, gracefully swishing back and forth as I stand or walk. Similarly, when I embody a bird, the feeling of freedom, openness, and expansion opens my body and my heart and gives me permission to express myself and take up space in the world. Snake embodiment gives me movement, sensuality, and fluidity. I love them all for different reasons.

We can all benefit from taking on some of these animalistic qualities and embodying them as we walk around in the world. It brings us added power, presence, attitude, freedom, and ability to attract attention.

We all have natural, predatory, animalistic instincts to move around on the world, just like animals in the wild. We just need to remember who we are and that we have that primal energy living inside of us.

CHAPTER 11

Pleasure is Healing

The Universe is interested in growing and sustaining our existence, and I believe it is invested in having the human race thrive, persist, and evolve. It rewards people who value and consider sacred the human body and its ability to create life, ideas, projects, movements, initiatives, and inventions. The sexual primal energy that we use to create human life is the same that we use to create an idea or a work of art -- and comes from the same energy center. A beautiful poem, a moving speech, an emotionally resonant song, or a baby; all come from the same energy.

As we cultivate this powerful energy, we increase our capacity to bring about the changes we wish to see in our lives and in the world. When we cultivate it by intentionally awakening our sexual energy, and when we have methods for storing and directing it with intention, we receive the by-products: more stamina, endurance, drive, determination, motivation, and passion. Our bodies and human spirits were designed with the capacity to develop and summon the skills and abilities necessary to keep the world spinning and ensure the continual survival of humankind.

Sexual desire is a powerful emotion — so powerful that people will take great risks and summon great courage to fulfill this desire. We can learn to harness this energy like fuel, propelling us toward other goals, in addition to procreation or sexual pleasure.

Most of us have been conditioned to believe that sexual desire is exclusively connected with sexual acts and procreation. Society lays thick shame on us for having too much sexual desire, the supposedly wrong kind, or even any desire at all. But, as we have learned by exploring the powers and energy that live in your pleasure power center, this energy is not just about sex. This energy is practical and productive: the feelings that get stirred up in our pleasure power center lead to our drive, creativity, enthusiasm, motivation, determination, and the fire and will to succeed. You can be turned on by ideas, music, people, nature, recognition, gratitude, success, art, movement, and life in general. You can be turned on in so many ways, and there is no reason to be ashamed of feeling turned on at any time or in any situation that does no harm to others.

When you feel turned on, you are tuned into your own power, energy, and aliveness. We don't want to make that go away. However, we don't always want to channel it toward sex, so we can learn to use the process of transmutation to express this energy in various creative and work-related ways. This fuel, when used with intention, can help you to use your divine primal energy to achieve your dreams and goals.

The continuation of humanity's existence requires us to procreate. Mother Nature also benefits when we use this sexual energy of desire not only to reproduce but to produce new ideas and creations.

Throughout this book, we have focused on feeling energy in our three main energy centers: head, heart, and Hara (pleasure power center). Sexual energy is associated with the Hara, emotions are associated with our heart, and intuition is associated with our head.

But we can harness that Hara energy and direct it toward the other two energy centers to help us achieve an energetic balance, heal our bodies with our life force energy, and use all three of these crucial energy centers together so we can create, receive guidance and wisdom, and take inspired action.

As a reminder, be sure you are grounded before harnessing this energy and performing the next exercise of energy circulation. We must be able to contain and hold the Hara energy before we can truly benefit from circulating it.

Circulating Your Life Force Energy

Everything that we have practiced thus far has been building up to us being able to perform the micro-cosmic orbit, a powerful energetic and life-force energy practice that allows you to generate and circulate the powerful energy from your pleasure power center throughout your body. This maneuver activates, energizes, and heals all of your energy centers.

Exercise: Micro-Cosmic Orbit

Find a comfortable seated position. Ensure that your spine is straight and that you are upright for this practice, so please refrain from practicing while lying down. Because this practice generates significant energy, I don't recommend doing it right before bed.

Begin to recall the gravity grounding technique from page 83 to begin to settle into your seated position. Focus on feeling your bottom touching the chair or floor, allowing it to fully support you, and allowing yourself to fully sink in while keeping your spine straight (sinking down and lengthening, not slouching.) Imagine that gravity is assisting you in sending any busy, scattered energy down from your headspace into your lower body, into your legs, and out through the tips of your toes.

Initiate your secret squeeze (as explained on page 74) by squeezing your pelvic control muscles. This helps your pleasure power center begin to generate life-force energy. Your secret squeezes act like a pump: they both generate and begin to move this energy from your power center into your upper energy centers. Perform at least five secret squeezes and begin to visualize a sphere of light suspended in your pelvic bowl. Imagine that sphere of light energy living and breathing inside of you, expanding and contracting as you breathe.

Now begin to send that light energy down to your perineum. Allow the energy to flow to the base of your spine, focusing your attention on the back of your spine. Use your secret squeezes and the power of your awareness and focus to send the energy up the back of your spine (known as the "governor channel" or "back channel" in Chinese medicine), sending it further up your back channel to the back of your pelvic center, solar plexus, and heart center until the energy reaches the top of your head. Imagine the energy travelling with just enough gentle momentum to send it up over the top of your head like a soft wave splashing over you. Allow the energy to cleanse your brain and head center.

Then, place the tip of your tongue on your soft palate, the soft area of the roof of your mouth that begins about an inch behind your teeth, where the roof of your mouth begins to curve up. This tongue placement closes your energy circuit and will help the energy to loop around to the front channel (or "conception channel" in Chinese medicine) of your body. Allow the energy to flow down over the top of your head, into the tip of your tongue, down your throat and into the front side of your body, over the front of your chest, torso, solar plexus, and pelvic area until it returns to your pleasure power center.

Continue circulating the energy in this looping manner; at the beginning of your practice, try for two minutes, then extend your practice with time. Enjoy the vibrant yet calm state this practice induces. It may take some time to experience this, but this practice will supply you with energy and balance.

If you find yourself feeling like the energy is stuck in certain places because it feels like something is blocking the energy from circulating, or there is tightness, a void, or a lack of sensation in certain parts of your system, you may still be experiencing some blockages. In that case, return to the Heart Clearing practices in Part Two to release any emotional wounds, traumas, or energy stuck in the body. This process of clearing your body and mental and emotional states while also becoming fully present in all three energy centers can take time. Be patient with yourself. This work takes consistent practice. You may also find that as you do the work and clear energy and blockages, you discover new ones that were hidden or are now ready to be processed. It is like peeling back the layers of an onion, and the deeper you go with the work, the deeper you'll be able to go.

Note: Part of the reason you don't want to practice this lying down is because you don't want the energy to get stuck in your heart center or in your head. You want to make sure it makes its way back to your pleasure power center.

If at any time you feel dizzy or lightheaded after your practice, spend at least five to ten minutes doing one or more of the grounding exercises beginning on page 81.

This practice of circulating and containing the energy will help you store your valuable life-force energy for yourself rather than dissipating or discharging it when the sensations seem too much to handle. For example, doing this practice will help you control your own energy so that you can extend sexual pleasure without climaxing too soon. This practice will also bring feelings of wholeness and balance by connecting your energy centers to each other so they can work together in unison. By moving your life-force energy throughout your body, you will also purify your energy and your organs. Use this practice to bring you back to balance when you feel scattered or are experiencing low levels of energy.

CHAPTER 12

Energetic Sweet Spot

If we imagine the sweet spot in terms of earth elements, the balance of physical and energetic presence would be the intermingling of the four elements of fire, earth, air, and water.

When you embody the strategies in Part Two, you can strengthen your fire and earth energies: intensity, physical presence, strength, groundedness, and power. But if you develop only these qualities, there is a good chance you will be perceived as either too intense or intimidating.

Similarly, if you develop only your energetic presence and its accompanying water and air elements without simultaneously embodying your fiery, passionate, intense energy, you may be seen as someone with their head in the clouds, walking around almost as though you are floating, very free, and spiritual, but as not really having your feet on the ground or in tune with your surroundings.

But when you intermingle these elements, you develop more aliveness and a strong yet heavenly quality to your presence.

Bring to mind your favorite actor and imagine them moving around on the set or on the screen. Chances are they appear very concrete and present, but they've also got that little something extra that you can't quite put your finger on — an aura of larger-than-life energy, charisma, or magnetism, that added special ingredient that balances their commanding physical presence with an airy radiance.

Power comes from being highly tuned in to your physical presence, which is possible when you have done your part in working to connect with your body and getting grounded with an animalistic type of presence. Grace comes from your ability to get into a state of flow and radiate your energetic presence.

When you can simultaneously embody both power and grace, you will automatically exude a magnetic presence: you will feel grounded and energized, you will make a good impression, and you will be calm, but you will also be able to show up with enthusiasm.

Relaxed Yet Alert

As much as I love practicing and teaching grounding, centering, and meditation, I've learned that if I am too calm, I won't have enough energy and enthusiasm to make a great impression. You don't want to be too calm when you have to be "on." In the sweet spot, you are centered and focused while also performing at a high level.

At the beginning of this work, people often think that being too nervous is a detriment to their presence. But don't worry about getting rid of all of your nervous energy — because many times, in the process you will end up getting rid of passion, enthusiasm, and the kind of excitement that enables you to show up and be absolutely amazing and magnetic.

A common pitfall of successfully managing anxiety is to mislabel excitement as nervousness. Excitement sometimes produces the same physical sensations in your body, like increased heart rate and fluttering sensations in the belly or chest. But these sensations often are simply symptoms that your body is preparing itself by supplying adrenaline, which can sometimes trick us into thinking that we are nervous or afraid. But if this energy is channeled in a productive way, it will increase your ability to be more animated. Many professional speakers have told me that they worry if they aren't having some of these symptoms before a speech because then they know they will lack the energy necessary to breathe life into their words.

Being too calm can equal being boring, too flat, not interested, disengaged — whether or not these are actual emotions you're feeling. Calmness can be a liability when it comes to making a good impression, standing out, and attracting people and opportunities.

I know a lot of yogis and meditators who are great at getting themselves calm, centered, and grounded, but when they are in front of a group or audience, while their energy may be soothing for some people, there is not enough energy to create the magnetism that will keep people interested. This is why we don't want to feel too secure or calm, like we've just stepped out of a bath or meditation. We also don't want to be so amped up that we can't center ourselves. There is a happy medium. A sweet spot. A perfect balance.

In the sweet spot, your centered, grounded energy is also matched by magnetism, passion, power and enthusiasm, conveying alertness, and presence.

EXERCISE: THREE ACTIVATION POINTS

One of the quickest ways to turn on your magnetic presence is to activate three main points within your body. I learned this trick from my mentor, Rachael Jayne Groover, author of Powerful and Feminine. You've already practiced how to strengthen and focus your energy on each of these areas individually. Now it's time to experience feeling and radiating from all three points at the same time.

If you are a woman:

Begin by putting all of your attention and awareness on your pleasure power center, the energetic space that is approximately two-and-a-half to three inches below your navel and in the center of your pelvic bowl. Imagine there is a sphere of light energy suspended there in this space and allow it to expand and contract with your breath as though it is living and breathing inside of you.

Once you sense that pulsating light in the center of your pelvic bowl, stay strong and centered there while also activating and sensing the back and forth and swirling flow of energy between your hips and throughout your entire pelvic bowl. Enjoy this flowy, open, sensual sensation as you feel the power and strength of your pleasure power center. Notice how powerful this feeling is when you combine these two practices.

Lastly, while maintaining both the movement of energy between your hips along with being grounded and centered in your womb space, add the final layer of this three-part activation by placing your attention on your heart space and chest area, imagining that you are radiating from your heart loving, warm, compassionate energy. Feel the sensations you can create in yourself simply by focusing on sending out loving, adoring energy to others, knowing that when you are in the presence of others, they will be able to feel it too.

If you are a man:

Begin by putting all of your attention and awareness on your pleasure power center, the energetic space that is approximately two inches below your navel and in the center of your pelvic region. Imagine there is a sphere of light energy suspended there in this space and allow it to expand and contract with your breath as though it is living and breathing inside of you.

Once you sense that pulsating light in the center of your pelvic region, stay strong and centered there while also projecting protective energy by expanding your chest and shoulders. Broaden your shoulders, feeling a nice, strong symmetry and strength across your chest as you send out protective energy. Feel a ray of energy coming from your chest and shoulders that has the power to protect the entire room.

For everyone:

Lastly, activate your heart center by imagining you are radiating loving, warm, compassionate energy from your heart. Feel the sensations you can create in yourself simply by focusing on sending out loving, adoring energy to others, knowing that when you are in the presence of others, they will be able to feel it too. Enjoy the power of this combination of energies as you feel the power and strength of your pleasure power center with a warm, giving, loving, compassionate heart.

Taking the Sweet Spot With You

If I say, in the middle of a workshop, "Okay, in just a minute, you are going to stand up and find a partner," most people will make some subtle or not so subtle adjustments in their body like sitting up straight or arching their back slightly. They start to get their body ready to stand up. But according to movement experts and according to the Alexander Method, our movements such as transitioning from sitting to standing should be more seamless and effortless. My Alexander Method teacher taught me not to slouch when I'm sitting so that when I get ready to stand up, all I have to do is push into my feet and initiate raising my body all at once instead of in jerky movements or leaning forward first or arching my back first. Sitting in an already "ready" and alert posture helps keep us aware, present, powerful and able to perform at our best with just a moment's notice.

Smooth transitions take practice but investing energy into transitions — from sitting to standing, from closed-eye meditations to meditative states that are sustainable while in the world and interacting with people — will help you stay centered no matter what comes your way.

Rather than meditating in your quiet room on your meditation cushion, try meditating in challenging conditions. While walking down a busy street in Los Angeles with my Tantra teacher, she explained that the most challenging places to practice meditation — busy streets, rush-hour subways, kids' soccer games — are also the best way to learn. They challenge your ability. She recalled practicing in the red-light district of Calcutta, India, with pungent smells in the air, raw sewage, people talking loudly, kids screaming, little cars zipping by, very high temperatures. Similarly, I once saw a video of a martial-arts expert and peak-performance coach meditating with his eyes open in the middle of Times Square. (I think this is a brilliant challenge for me and my clients, so it's on my bucket list.)

Intense sensory input like this help you elevate your meditation practice — it takes more skill to still the mind, tune in, connect with yourself and your universal source energy, or higher power while you're in the midst of chaos. Perhaps start by going to a park, in your home with loud music or with the television on.

We can learn to maintain our meditative states by practicing how we transition from our meditations back to the real world.

Sometimes when I'm leading a meditation or visualization, I like to invite my client to imagine they are opening up their eyes before they actually open them so that they can begin to transition. This allows them to practice holding their meditative state with the added visual stimulation and despite the temptation to revert to their previous state of busyness or rushing.

EXERCISE: PRACTICE TRANSITIONING

Here is a simple exercise to incorporate into any closed-eye meditation practice or visualization.

Keep your eyes closed at the conclusion of your meditation practice.

Allow yourself at least one minute to prepare yourself to open your eyes and allow yourself to start adjusting to the idea of being met with the visual stimulation that you have had the opportunity to be free of during your practice.

Begin by starting to remember what your environment and surroundings look like. Picture them with as much vivid detail as you can.

Then, imagine that you are opening your eyes without really doing it and notice if you sense any change in your heart rate or an increase in nervousness or anxiety by envisioning that you are re-entering the physical world. If you do notice an undesirable shift, return to the practices that helped you achieve your meditative state until you feel calm and relaxed again. Then try to imagine your surroundings once again.

Now you are ready to slowly begin to enter the real world by opening your eyes ever so slightly, maybe only ten percent of the way open. Take in the light and stimulation that your senses take in and practice maintaining your state of being.

If you still feel relatively grounded and centered, continue to open your eyes completely, but at a very slow, steady pace, giving yourself at least five seconds to fully open your eyes.

Remain still. Don't move your body or your eye gaze. Simply look straight ahead and take in the sights and sounds for at least five seconds.

Then begin to shift your eye gaze or slowly start to look around your room.

Take just as much time to sit or stand up as you did in the process of opening your eyes to slowly transition to a more active physical stance.

Check in with your physical, mental, and emotional state to see if you have retained the benefits of your meditation practice up to this point.

Proceed to start walking around and moving about your day with the same mindful presence and attention to retaining the state of being that you achieved during your meditation practice. Naturally, you will begin to operate at a faster pace and with time will be able to extend and maintain the same emotional, physical, and mental state that you are able to achieve during meditation.

EXERCISE: STRIKING THE PERFECT ENERGETIC BALANCE

Practice striking a balance between your physical and energetic presence.

Embodying the four earth elements can help you achieve the magnetic state that will help you look and feel confident. Let's practice embodying aspects of these elements, first in pairs, then we'll practice bringing them all together.

Earth energy corresponds to stability, strength and feelings of concrete presence.

Fire Energy corresponds to energy that is focused, concentrated, direct, hot, and passionate.

First, practice emphasizing your physical presence and fiery energy. Combining fire and earth energies creates a solid, anchored, and strong physical presence.

Tilt the balance toward your physical presence by focusing on a strong, grounded feeling in your legs and feet. Imagine that you are a 1,000-year-old tree with roots that go 100 feet into the ground. Begin by practicing being very physically present in your entire body, inviting feelings of strength, assertiveness, heaviness, rigidity, and stability. For a few moments, focus on feeling this solid physicality in your arms and hands.

Move them like a robot would, in short rigid fashion. Do this for at least 30 seconds to get the gist of it. Then, extend that movement to the rest of your body: do a very physical walk that concentrates all of your energy in the cells of your body. This usually creates a heavy and deliberate movement that feels like having cement in your veins.

Now, shake and wiggle your body around to shed that extremely physical energy.

Next, practice tilting the balance toward total energetic presence. It's very light and fluid. For this variation, you'll focus on embodying the water and air elements.

Water energy signifies compassionate, magnetic, soothing, smooth, flexible energy.

Air energy signifies cool, flowing energy.

Practice inviting the water and air energies to combine by gently and lightly waving your hands through the air, in a light, graceful, celestial manner. Just let them go where they want, almost weightlessly. Free your energy, making it so light that it feels like it's actually wafting away from your body.

Extend this into your walk after you've practiced for at least 30 seconds. When you walk in this very energetic state, you may feel like your head is in the clouds or like you're walking on air. Just notice the contrast.

Shake off the excess airy energy and rest your body.

> *Now, try entering a balance of all four elements. First, see if you can move your hands in that middle range where you are half physical and half energetic, embodying all four elements at the same time. This should create a mixture that feels good in your body and helps you enter that sweet spot where you've got just enough movement, flow, and flexibility to balance and merge with your hot, fiery intensity, creating a powerful and magnetic presence.*
>
> *Again, begin by inviting and embodying all four elements just in your arms and hands initially to find that magic balance, the perfect sweet spot.*
>
> *Now try it with your whole body by walking around in your energetic sweet spot. When you notice yourself walking around and showing up in the world with too much concrete presence and not enough flowy, magic energy, make an adjustment in your presence to invite more air and water. Conversely, if you find yourself feeling like you're floating around and very in touch with your energy but lacking some grounding and fiery, stable presence, invite more earth and fire energy.*

At the beginning of these practices, it may feel like you're trying to do several things at once, and that too much thinking is required, which may seem to contradict the end goal getting out of your head. But trust the process and know that even though it may seem a bit challenging at first, with continued practice it will become easier to adopt these states of being without thinking too much about what you're doing. It's like learning to ride a bike or play an instrument: in the beginning, it may feel a little choppy and will require mind energy, but eventually you will be able to do it like it's second nature and will be able to slip into your energetic sweet spot whenever you choose.

Epilogue

"I'm on my way to the hospital."

I pressed my phone to my ear, trying to understand my mom's words, which were barely intelligible through her tears.

"Mom? Mom, what's going on?" I sat in my car outside the hot yoga studio, my pulse pounding even harder than it had during class. What was going on?

Finally, she was able to say, "It's my brother, Andy. The doctors say it doesn't look good." My heart dropped. I pictured him wearing his green-and-yellow Green Bay Packers bomber jacket and wondered if he was scared, if he was alone, and what exactly had happened. I was an hour away. How fast could I get there?

By the time I dashed into the hospital, my mom's face was twisted in grief. My uncle had suffered a brain aneurysm; he could no longer breathe on his own, and there wasn't much they could do. Everyone was in shock. It all happened so suddenly. Nobody was prepared for this. He was only 56 years old and each of his children and his four younger sisters, all of whom adored him, were devastated. The energy of that waiting room, filled with our family, was heavy. He passed on before the night was over.

He had been kind to me as long as I could remember. He loved taking me and my cousins fishing, blaring the stereo in the car, and telling jokes on the way to the river. We laughed, we sang, and he taught us how to bait a hook. Now he was gone.

When it came time to make funeral arrangements, my mom asked me if I'd deliver the eulogy. I couldn't say no, even though the thought of putting something together so quickly amidst all the emotion that was swirling around seemed a little overwhelming.

I took my responsibility very seriously. Our family was grieving, but I had to get to work. I'd never given a eulogy before. I had only a couple of days to prepare, which made me nervous. Andy had brought so much to this world — his spirit, gifts, blessings, smiles, jokes, and lessons — and I was responsible for making sure that everyone who came to remember him had the opportunity to reflect on his special presence in our lives.

I had a feeling that Andy would not want us to focus on our grief and the sudden hole in our family. He'd want us to smile and remember our favorite moments with him. He'd be happy if we found ways to keep alive the parts of him that lived in our hearts.

With only a few days to get ready, I didn't have time to obsess over the trivial things that I normally worried about when preparing to speak to a group of people: *"Will I make a good impression? Will they like me? Will they think I'm smart? Will they think I'm qualified?"*

As I usually am while preparing a speech, I was nervous, but in a different way. This wasn't for a client, so I didn't need high scores on a speaker-evaluation sheet. I wanted to do a good job to make sure that the message landed in the hearts of the people sitting in those pews at the church.

It wasn't about me this time.

I sat on my bedroom floor listening to *Stairway to Heaven*, one of Andy's favorite songs, and started making a list of things that reminded me of him.

When it was time for me to walk up the aisle of that church in downtown Santa Fe, I stepped up to the pulpit and stood behind the lectern. I wasn't afraid I might cry. I welcomed the emotion. I gave myself permission to fully surrender to the feelings behind the message.

I spoke about what Andy loved: guitars, the Green Bay Packers, fishing, and classic rock music. I spoke about his intelligence and wit, and his loving dedication to his family. He raised his daughters as a single dad for most of their childhood. He'd accomplished so much in his life, but most of all, he had one of the kindest hearts I've ever encountered.

After the service, my family and I went outside to greet everyone who had come to pay their respects. Everyone I spoke to — even people I'd never met, but who loved Andy — expressed their gratitude for helping them remember him in such a special way. Their reactions and responses let me know that I had done my job.

Having the privilege of delivering my Uncle Andy's eulogy was something I'll never forget. I had the chance to offer my own gift in service of his memory and in gratitude for his life.

Speaking in front of Andy's family and friends also taught me a humble lesson about primal presence. In the face of death, I learned that it's not really about making a good impression, or getting high marks on an evaluation sheet, or becoming a social media influencer.

Primal presence is about vulnerability, rawness, and emotion. People are drawn to real people, not perfect people.

I used to want to be a polished and professional speaker, but now, mostly I want to make people feel something. I want to spark a feeling of hope, understanding, acceptance, or inspiration in those I connect with.

You don't have to be a speaker to communicate in a way that moves people on a deep level. It doesn't matter what business you're in or what you're selling — if you can convey why you do what you do with emotion, vulnerability, power, and compassion, you will draw more people to you.

People want to feel something. We want to be reminded that we're alive. If you're alive and emotionally transparent, unafraid to let your voice shake, to let an occasional tear fall, to be human, you will be powerful and magnetic.

Each of us is most powerful when we communicate in a way that focuses less on ourselves and more on creating genuine connection.

On this journey we have explored how to invite unconditional self-love, how to remember what it feels like to truly be alive, and how to exude the power of our true divine nature. One of the best side effects of developing a powerful and magnetic presence is that you will affect others simply by being yourself. Without saying a word, people will know they are in the presence of someone who is alive and owning their power in a rarely seen manner. When you hold this kind of space, exuding power and compassion, you communicate the unspoken message that they, too, are more powerful and perfect than they know. This is the true gift of going through all of this work, having the privilege of being a living, breathing example of what it is like to come alive.

Looking out at all those faces of the people in the church that day, I remember their eyes the most. They all looked beautiful to me. They were in a state of love, compassion, tenderness, and without knowing it, they were exercising one of our fundamental practices: the vulnerability and compassion that radiates from an open heart.

No one that day puffed out their chest, trying to stand out and attract attention. They had shown up to honor Andy. When we are forced to remember how delicate and precious life is, heart-opening naturally occurs. In normal, everyday life, we are usually on guard in some respects, but funerals have a way of giving us perspective and an opportunity to reflect on our own lives and ask the questions:

"What do I want people to remember most about me?"

"How do I want to make people feel?

With your aliveness, fiery spirit, and compassionate heart, you have the tools to make your presence known and affect the energy of every room you walk into.

Carl W. Buehner said, "They may forget what you said - but they will never forget how you made them feel."

So how do YOU want to make people feel?

Acknowledgements

I acknowledge with great respect and gratitude:

- Rachael Jayne Groover and her Art of Feminine Presence body of work, which greatly influenced my work and this book.

- Master Hongik, Master Keum Dao, Master Chung Suk, and Ilchi Lee for the Korean energetic principles that helped me deepen my connection with my body and master the energetic principles that have changed my life and equipped me to better serve my clients.

- Psalm Isadora for introducing me to Tantric practice and helping me release the chains that were holding me back.

- Jack Canfield and the Canfield Community including Natalie, Joe, Sharon, Shawn, Amanda, Nora, Alice, Derek, Josee, Michael, Dr. Deb, Jesse, and Amina for helping me love myself enough to be myself.

- Jinlen, Jennifer and Khara for creating the most beautiful circle unconditional support, respect, safety and love that I've experienced.

- Bo Eason and Jean-Louis Rodrigue for reminding me of my primal power.

- Jennifer Wilson, Bernadette Vadurro, Tamera Loerzel, and Craig Valentine for making me a better speaker.

- Jennifer Gandin Le for helping me birth this book with loving guidance and expertise.

- My husband Brain for supporting me in all my endeavors no matter how crazy they seemed.

- My daughter Talia for teaching me and lighting me up with her old-soul wisdom and unconditional love.

- My sister Alyssa for being my most beautiful, enthusiastic cheerleader.

- Mom and Dad for always believing in me and making me feel special since the day I was born.

About the Author

Michelle Baca is a speaker, author, and coach who helps people communicate with confidence, power, and influence. She co-authored the best-selling book "The Soul of Success" with Jack Canfield, creator of the "Chicken Soup for the Soul" series.

Through her work as a Level II Art of Feminine Presence Certified Teacher and her former consulting for ConvergenceCoaching, she encourages and inspires people to achieve personal and professional success. Michelle incorporates energetic and embodiment principles and tantric techniques to help her clients stay centered, inspired, energized, and capable of handling anything that comes their way.

As an outgoing introvert and recovering overthinker, Michelle especially loves to work with people who tend to worry, obsess, and overanalyze get out of their heads and into their bodies so that they can fully express themselves with more ease and authenticity.

She lives in Albuquerque, NM, with her husband and daughter.

www.ingramcontent.com/pod-product-compliance
Lightning Source LLC
Chambersburg PA
CBHW020331110726

47898CB00003B/829

* 9 7 8 1 6 4 1 8 4 1 1 8 4 *